THE
ELSON READERS

BOOK THREE
(*Revision of Elson Primary School Reader, Book Three*)

William H. Elson
AUTHOR OF ELSON GOOD ENGLISH SERIES

PUBLISHER'S NOTE

Recognizing the need to return to more traditional principles in education, Lost Classics Book Company is republishing forgotten late 19th and early 20th century literature and textbooks to aid parents in the education of their children.

This edition of *The Elson Readers—Book Three* was reprinted from the 1920 copyright edition. The text has been updated and edited only where necessary. Spelling and punctuation have been updated in works of prose, but not in poetry—these things being the prerogative of the poet.

We have included a glossary and pronunciation guide of more than 493 terms at the end of the book to encourage children to look up words they don't know.

The Elson Readers—Book Three has been assigned a reading level of 750L. More information concerning this reading level assessment may be attained by visiting www.lexile.com.

Library of Congress Catalog Card Number: 2005928904
ISBN 978-1-890623-17-3
Part of
The Elson Readers
Nine Volumes: *Primer* through *Book Eight*
ISBN 978-1-890623-23-4

On the Cover:
Joseph, Overseer of the Pharoahs by
Sir Lawrence Alma-Tadema (1836-1912)
Private Collection/Bridgeman Art Library

WILLIAM H. ELSON

———•———

In the early 1930s, William Harris Elson capped off a successful career as an educator and author of textbook readers by creating the "Fun with Dick and Jane" pre-primer readers with co-author William Scott Gray. Dick and Jane, their families, friends, and pets entered the popular culture as symbols of childhood, and the books themselves became synonymous with the first steps in learning to read.

In 1909 The Elson Grammar School Reader, the first in a nine-volume series of school readers, appeared to immediate success. The Elson Readers, which Lost Classics Book Company is reprinting, were among Elson's earliest creations and go well beyond the scope of the "Dick and Jane" books. Following a carefully planned model that stresses both improving comprehension and developing appreciation for literature, Elson organized the books in a way that built on the understanding and skills taught in earlier volumes.

Assisting Elson on the series were publishing house writers Lura Runkel and Christine Keck. Runkel helped on the primer and the first and second volume, while Keck worked on the fifth through the eighth volume. Obviously both writers were schooled well in Elson's methodology, as the series displays remarkable consistency and accuracy throughout the entire set of books.

Through the eighth grade, or ages 13 to 14, each succeeding book in the Elson Readers series introduces students to increasingly complex genres and better writers. The result of using the series as intended is better reading skills and comprehension as well as a growing appreciation for good writing. But the books are so thorough that they may be used individually and still advance a student's understanding and appreciation for the types of writing in a particular volume.

Born on November 22, 1854, in Carroll County, Ohio, Elson lived through a tumultuous period, becoming an educator who helped usher in numerous innovations. Although he did not receive his A.B. degree from Indiana University until 1895, he was active as a schoolteacher and as a school administrator for many years before, beginning with his first teaching assignment in 1881. By 1907 he had established the first technical high school in the nation in Cleveland, Ohio, where he served as school superintendent from 1906-12.

Elson's contributions to teaching children to read and appreciate literature included not only the *Elson Readers* but many other series for which he served as primary author or editor, including *Good English* (3 vols., 1916); *Child-Library Readers* (9 vols., 1923-34); and *Elson Junior Literature* (2 vols., 1932). By the time of his death on February 2, 1935, his books had sold over fifty million copies and were in use in 34 countries on every continent.

Besides helping to create the engaging "Fun with Dick and Jane" books, William Harris Elson implemented a developmental approach to learning reading skills that still works extremely well. Lost Classics Book Company's republication of this volume from the *Elson Readers* provides access to a book that will provide children with a delightful and effective learning experience.

David E. Vancil, Ph.D.
Indiana State University

Biographical Dictionary of American Educators. 3 Vols. Edited by John F. Ohles. Westport, CT: Greenwood Press, 1978. Alphabetical entry.

The National Cyclopaedia of American Biography. Volume 26. New York: James T. White & Co., 1937. Pp. 367-68.

Contents

6

PREFACE

Book Three of the *Elson Readers* introduces the child to stories and poems of compelling interest and to some of the great story-tellers, ancient and modern. The book recognizes that the child at this stage is in the golden age of pure fancy, and that stories which appeal to his imagination are best suited not only to interest him in reading, but also to interpret for him his own experiences. The world of reality, however, is not overlooked, for the magic realm of nature is given abundant recognition.

This book is distinctive for the many selections that impress a wholesome influence of high ethical ideals, particularly the ideal of *service*. Not only are there stories from the past—fairy tales, fables, and folk tales—but also present-day stories, rich in ideals of home and country, heroism, and helpfulness to others—ideals to which the World Wars have given new meaning that the school reader should perpetuate. There are stories and poems of the flag, of Washington and Lincoln, and of the Red Cross, as well as selections suited to festival occasions—Thanksgiving, Christmas, New Year, Easter, Arbor and Bird Day, and Columbus Day. There is something for every day's needs and for all the children.

The many action stories in this book adapt it to the purposes of rapid silent reading—a project of a most important kind. (See "Suggestions for Silent Reading" in "Helps to Study.") Several of the selections are presented in dramatized form, while many others lend themselves admirably to this treatment, thus offering project material of another excellent type.

In the preparation of this book particular attention has been given to simplicity of treatment, not only in vocabulary, but also in the story-element, the plot. The "Helps to Study" contain questions and suggestions that make clear the main idea, stimulate thinking, and lead to habits of observation and inquiry.

A "Word List" for spelling, pronunciation, and meaning, provides a basis for systematically increasing the child's vocabulary.

7

Summer fading, winter comes—
Frosty mornings, tingling thumbs,
Window robins, winter rooks,
And the picture story-books.

       —*Robert Louis Stevenson*

THE HARE AND THE HEDGEHOG

THE RUDE LITTLE HARE

One summer morning a little hedgehog was sitting at the door of his home. He was a merry little fellow who wished everybody to be happy.

"I think I'll just run over to the field and take a look at our turnips," he said to his wife.

"I hope you won't meet any of those rude hares," said little Mrs. Hedgehog. "Yesterday they were in their cabbage patch when our little ones and I walked by. They laughed at our short legs, and said it must be stupid to be so slow."

9

"Do not mind them, my dear. A hedgehog is as good as a hare any day. I'll be back soon," said the little hedgehog as he started off.

Just as he reached the turnip field he met a little hare. Now the hare thought himself a very fine fellow, indeed, because he could run like the wind. He was proud and ill-tempered, too.

When the little hedgehog saw the hare, he said in his pleasantest manner, "Good morning, Neighbor Hare."

The hare did not answer his polite greeting, but said in a very rude manner, "Why are you in the fields so early this morning?"

"Oh, I'm just taking a walk," answered the little hedgehog pleasantly.

"Taking a walk!" said the hare with a laugh. "What fun can it be to walk with such queer, short legs? I saw your wife and little ones yesterday, and I thought I should die laughing at them."

This rude speech made the little hedgehog very angry. "I suppose you think your long legs are much better than my short ones," he said. "But if you will run a race with me, I'll show you that my legs are quite as good as yours."

"That sounds like a joke," said the hare. "But I'll race with you right now. We'll race down the furrows between your fine turnips. You run in one furrow and I'll run in another, and we shall soon see who will reach the other end first. We may as well start at once, and get the race over."

"Not so fast," said the hedgehog. "I must go home and get some breakfast first. In half an hour I'll be here again."

The hare said that he would wait for him, and the hedgehog started home. "That rude hare is too proud of his long legs," said the little hedgehog to himself. "I'll teach him that it does not pay to boast."

The Race

When he reached home he found his wife, and asked her to help him play a joke on the hare. On the way to the turnip field he told her just what he wanted her to do. "You must hide at the far end of the furrow," he said. "Just before the hare reaches there you must pop your head up and say, 'I am here first!' You and I look so much alike that the hare will think I have beaten him."

The hedgehog's wife laughed and laughed at the joke they would play on the proud hare.

Soon they reached the field, and the little hedgehog placed his wife at the far end of the furrow. Then he went to the other end, where he found the hare waiting for him.

"Let's start at once," said the proud hare, "and get this foolish race over."

"I am quite ready," said the little hedgehog as he took his place in his furrow.

The hare hopped to the next furrow and took his place. Then he counted, "One, two, three, go!" and away he went like the wind.

The little hedgehog ran only a few steps and

then he lay quite still among the leaves. The hare thought that the hedgehog was still running.

Just before the hare reached the far end of his furrow, the hedgehog's wife popped up her head and said, "I am here first!"

The hare stood still in wonder. "Well, this is strange!" he said.

"Not strange at all," said the hedgehog's wife.

"Let's race back," said the little hare. "You cannot beat me again."

"I'm very willing," said the hedgehog's wife.

So the hare turned quickly and ran back through his furrow even faster than at first.

But just before he reached the other end, the little hedgehog popped up his head and said, "I am here first!"

"I can't understand this at all," said the surprised hare.

"It's just as simple as A, B, C," said the hedgehog.

"Well, let's try again," said the hare.

"As often as you please," said the little hedgehog. "I feel just as fresh as when we started."

"One, two, three!" said the hare, and he was off. But when he reached the other end, the hedgehog's wife put up her head and said, "Well, I am here first again! Neighbor Hare, you begin to look tired."

The hare did not answer her, but started back again. Up and down his furrow he went, just seventy-three times, but each time one hedgehog or the other said, "I am here first!"

At last the hare was too tired to run any more, so he hopped slowly and sadly away.

The little hedgehogs laughed and laughed as they ate a fine juicy turnip. "Brains are better than legs, my dear," said the happy little hedgehog to his happy little wife.

—Grimm

OLD HORSES KNOW BEST

Once an old horse and a young horse were going down a hill. Each horse was drawing a cart piled high with jars and dishes. The old horse went down so slowly and carefully that the young horse laughed at him.

"How slowly you walk!" he said. "That would do if you were going up-hill, but this is down-hill. I'll show you how to go down in a hurry."

Then the young horse started quickly down the hill. The heavy cart rolled after him, and pushed against him so hard that he had to go faster and faster.

On he went, over stones and ruts! At last the horse and the cart and all the jars and dishes went tumbling into a ditch. The young horse looked at the over-turned cart and the broken dishes.

"I see that I have some things to learn yet," he said. "Old horses know best, after all."

—Russian Tale

THE MISER

Once upon a time there was a miser who hid his gold at the foot of a tree in his garden. Every week he dug it up and looked at it.

One night a robber dug up the gold and ran away with it. The next morning, when the miser came to look at his treasure, he found only the empty hole.

Then he raised such a cry of sorrow that the neighbors ran to find out what the trouble was. In great grief, he told them of his loss.

"Did you ever use any of the gold?" asked one of his neighbors.

"No," answered the miser, "but I looked at it every week."

"Then come every week and look at the hole," said the neighbor. "That will do you just as much good as to look at the gold."

—Aesop

THE DOG AND THE HORSE

A dog and a horse once lived in the same farm-yard. In the spring the fields around the farm were green with grain; in summer they were yellow with ripening wheat; in autumn they were brown with the harvest.

As the neighbors passed by this farm, they always said, "Stefan has a fine farm. He is a lucky man."

One day, when the dog heard these words, he said to the horse, "Of course Stefan has a fine farm. That is because I work so hard. In the daytime I keep the cattle out of the fields of grain. At night I guard the house and barns so that thieves cannot enter.

"But what do you do? I have never seen you do anything but plow, or draw a cart; and you sleep all night. The farm could get along without you."

"What you say about yourself is true," answered the horse. "You do keep the cattle out of the fields of grain, and you do guard the barns and the house at night. But did you ever stop to think that if I did not plow the fields, there would be no grain here for you to guard?

"Stefan would have no wheat and oats and barley in his barns. He would not need to keep a watchdog, and you would have no home. Perhaps I had better live in the farmyard a little longer. What do you think about it now?"

And for once, the dog had nothing to say.

—*Russian Tale*

THE FOX AND THE CROW

Once upon a time a crow, with a piece of cheese in her beak, was sitting in a tree. A fox saw her and thought, "How good that cheese looks!"

So he walked up to the foot of the tree and called out, "Good-morning, Madam Crow! How beautiful your feathers are! I am sure that you have a fine voice, too. Will you not sing a song for me?"

The crow was so pleased at this praise that she began to "caw." But the moment she opened her mouth to sing, the cheese fell to the ground.

"You need not sing any more, Madam Crow," said the fox, snapping up the cheese. "All that I wanted was the cheese."

"How foolish I was to let him flatter me!" said the crow.

—*Aesop*

THE CLOWN AND THE FARMER

Once a clown at a circus made a noise so much like a pig's squeal that he fooled the people.

Just then a farmer called out, "That does not sound like a pig's squeal! Tomorrow I will show you what a pig's squeal is like."

The people laughed at him, but the next day he came back, put his head down, and pretended to squeal. At once the people shouted, "That does not sound like a pig !"

"Ha! Ha! Ha!" laughed the farmer, holding out a little pig which he had hidden behind him. "You do not know a pig's squeal when you hear it."

—Old Tale

WHY THE RABBIT'S TAIL IS SHORT

Once upon a time the rabbit's tail was long, but now it is short. And this is how it happened.

A rabbit one day sat by a swamp, looking at the juicy plants on the other side. They were the only things to eat that he could see. He wanted to cross the swamp, but he could not swim.

Just then a lazy old alligator poked his nose above the water. "I might ask him to take me across," said the rabbit to himself. "But I am afraid that he is too proud to carry me, because he can walk and swim, too. Perhaps I can get across the swamp by playing a trick upon him. I will try it."

"You look warm, Friend Rabbit," said the alligator. "Why don't you come into the water? It is cool here." Now the alligator knew very well that the rabbit could not swim.

"I am not warm at all," said the rabbit, "but I am a little hungry. You see there are a great many rabbits in the world. There are hundreds and hundreds of them. So, of course, it takes a great many green leaves to feed us. Oh, yes! Friend Alligator, we are a very large family. There are many more rabbits than alligators."

"How foolish you are!" cried the alligator, angrily. "Why, there are thousands and thousands of alligators in the world! There are more than a hundred alligators in this swamp! Can you find a hundred rabbits in the woods?"

"Certainly I can!" said the rabbit. "I'll count the alligators, and then you may count the rabbits. Call the alligators together. Make a line of them across the swamp so that I can hop out upon their backs and count them."

So the old alligator called and called. Up from the swamp came alligators, big ones and little ones. The old alligator made them into a line right across the swamp, just like a bridge.

"Now count them, Friend Rabbit," he said. "If there are not more than a hundred alligators here, you may eat me!"

The rabbit hopped upon the alligator-bridge. As he went from one to another, he counted them, "One, two, three, four, five," and so on, up to a hundred. Yes! there were more than a hundred.

By the time he had counted the last alligator, the sly rabbit was on the other side of the swamp.

"I'll call the rabbits together some other day, when I am not so hungry," he called back to the old alligator. "Good-bye! Who is foolish now?" he said with a laugh.

But the rabbit laughed too soon. For one of the alligators caught the end of the rabbit's tail in his great jaws, and bit it off.

Since then rabbits' tails have always been short.

—*Old Southern Tale*

THE SIMPLETON

ACT I

Time—Long Ago

Place—A Country Road

Persons:

SIMPLETON

FIRST FARMER   SECOND FARMER

[*Simpleton walks along, jingling money in his pocket. He meets First Farmer with a basket.*]

SIMPLETON. Good-day, Sir! What is in your basket?

FIRST FARMER. [*Rudely.*] Nothing for you!

[*Simpleton walks away, jingling his money.*]

FIRST FARMER. [*Calling after Simpleton.*] What is that noise I hear?

SIMPLETON. [*Stopping.*] Oh, that is just my money jingling.

FIRST FARMER. How did you get money enough to make such a merry sound?

SIMPLETON. Oh, my brothers gave me twenty pieces of money. They say that I am a simpleton, so they sent me away from home.

FIRST FARMER. Oho! Well, see! This is a goose in my basket, a wonderful goose, a splendid goose! I am taking it to market.

SIMPLETON. [*Peeping into the basket.*] Will you sell your goose for twenty pieces of money?

FIRST FARMER. Well, it is worth more than that, but I will let you have it.

[*Simpleton buys the goose and goes on. After a while he meets Second Farmer.*]

SIMPLETON. [*Pointing.*] Who lives in that beautiful palace on the hill?

SECOND FARMER. What a simpleton you must be! Have you never heard of the king's palace? Our great king lives there.

SIMPLETON. Oho! I will take my goose to the palace and give it to the king.

[*He goes on his way, singing merrily.*]

ACT II

Time—THE SAME DAY
Place—THE KING'S PALACE

Persons:

SIMPLETON

FIRST SERVANT   SECOND SERVANT

[*Simpleton knocks at the palace door. First Servant opens it.*]

FIRST SERVANT. What do you want?

SIMPLETON. I want to see the king. I have a present for him.

FIRST SERVANT. Oh, indeed! I must see your present before it can be taken to the king.

Simpleton. Well, you may see it. [*Opens basket.*]

FIRST SERVANT. That is a fine goose. But half of it is mine!

SIMPLETON. What do you mean?

FIRST SERVANT. You must be a simpleton! I am keeper of the palace door. Half of everything that is carried through it must be given to me.

SIMPLETON. But this is a present for the king. I cannot take half a goose to the king.

FIRST SERVANT. That is true, but I will tell you what to do. Take the goose to the king. He will reward you. Promise me that I shall have half of whatever the king gives you.

SIMPLETON. Very well! I promise you.

[*First Servant takes Simpleton to the stairs, where they meet Second Servant.*]

SECOND SERVANT. Here, here! Not so fast. Who are you? What is your business?

SIMPLETON. I have a present for the king.

SECOND SERVANT. What is it? You cannot go farther until I see what it is.

SIMPLETON. [*Opening the basket:*] It is a goose.

SECOND SERVANT. It is a splendid goose! But I am the keeper of these stairs, and half of everything that goes up them must be given to me.

SIMPLETON. But I cannot give half a goose to the king. Let me see. This keeper of the door says the king may reward me. Suppose I give you half of my reward?

SECOND SERVANT. Do you promise it to me?

SIMPLETON. Yes, I promise it.

SECOND SERVANT. Then I will lead you to the king.

[*Simpleton and Servants go up the stairs.*]

ACT III

Time—A FEW MOMENTS LATER

Place—THE THRONE ROOM OF THE PALACE

Persons:

THE KING	SECOND SERVANT
SIMPLETON	THIRD SERVANT
FIRST SERVANT	OTHER SERVANTS

[*Second Servant leads Simpleton to the king. First Servant follows.*]

King. What have you in that basket?

SIMPLETON. [*Bowing low.*] I have brought a gift for Your Majesty.

King. Open the basket. [*To Simpleton, as the goose is uncovered.*] This is indeed a goose fit for a king. You shall be rewarded for your gift. Choose wisely, and you shall have whatever you ask.

SECOND SERVANT. [*Whispering to Simpleton*] Ask for a bag of gold.

FIRST SERVANT. [*Whispering to Simpleton.*] Ask for a box full of jewels.

SIMPLETON. I will ask for neither gold nor jewels. I ask for no reward but a sound beating, O King.

[*All the Servants cry out in surprise.*]

KING. A sound beating! I thought all lads had plenty of beatings without asking for them. Come, change your mind! Do you call that a wise choice?

SIMPLETON. [*Bowing low.*] I wish nothing for a reward but a sound beating.

KING. Then it shall be as you say. [To Third Servant.] Take this lad away and give him fifty strokes.

SIMPLETON. Wait! This reward is not mine. I must not take it. The servant who guards the door made me promise to give him half my reward, before he would open the door. I had to promise the other half to the servant who guards the stairs, before he would lead me here. It is only right that I should keep my promises. It would not be honest for me to take the reward; these servants must have it.

[*The king and the servants stare in wonder. Then, as they begin to understand Simpleton's strange wish, they nod their heads.*]

KING. [*To First and Second Servants, sternly.*] Is this the way you treat strangers? [*To Third Servant.*] Each claimed half of the reward. Very well! The reward is a beating of fifty strokes. Take these two servants out and give each of them half of the reward.

[*First Servant and Second Servant are led out. The other servants laugh aloud at the joke on the two servants. Even the king smiles.*]

ALL. Ha! ha! Ho! ho! ho!

KING. As for you, my lad, tell me your name.

SIMPLETON. My brothers call me Simpleton. They sent me away from home.

KING. You shall stay here in my palace. I need just such simpletons as you.

—Grimm

THE STONE-CUTTER

A stone-cutter named Tawara once lived in Japan. Every day he went to the mountain with his mallet and chisel. There he cut blocks of stone and polished them for the builders.

One day he carried a block of stone to a rich man's house, where he saw all sorts of beautiful furnishings. " Oh! I wish I were rich! " said Tawara. "Then I, too, could sleep in a soft bed."

Now the fairy of the mountains heard this wish and granted it. When Tawara reached his home, he stared in wonder! A beautiful house stood where his poor little hut had been! That night he slept on a bed as soft as down.

"I will work no more," said Tawara to himself. So for a time he lived happily in the great house with old furnishings all about him, and with plenty of rich food to eat.

But one day he saw a carriage go by, drawn by two snow-white horses. In it sat a prince, with a great umbrella held over his head by a servant.

Tawara forgot his good fortune. "Oh, I wish I were a prince!" he said. "I want to ride in a carriage, with a great umbrella over my head."

No sooner had he made his wish than he found that he was a prince. He rode in his carriage through the streets, with a great umbrella held over his head.

"Now I am happy," said Tawara to himself.

For a time he was happy. But one hot summer day, when he went into his garden, he found that all of his roses were drooping. "Why do these flowers droop their heads?" he asked.

His servants bowed before him. "It is the sun; O Prince," they said. " We have watered the garden, just as you told us to do, but the heat of the sun is too great."

"Is the sun greater than I am?" cried Tawara. " I wish I were the sun!"

No sooner had he made his wish than he found that he was the sun. He burned the rice fields and made the flowers droop their heads with his fierce heat.

"Now at last I am great!" he said to himself, proudly. "No one is so mighty as I."

But one day a thick black cloud covered his face. When he found that he could not pierce it with his strongest rays, he became unhappy again. "The cloud is mightier than I," he said. "I wish I were the cloud!"

No sooner had he made his wish than he found that he was the cloud. He hid the sun, and sent rain to the earth. The rice fields became green again, and the flowers bloomed.

Day after day the cloud poured down rain. The rivers overflowed their banks; villages and towns were washed away. But one thing he could not move. The great stone of the mountainside stood firm.

He was very angry. "Is the stone of the mountainside stronger than I am?" he cried. "I wish I were that stone!"

No sooner had he made his wish than he found that he was the stone. "Now at last I am happy," he said. "I am greater than sun and cloud. I cannot be burned and I cannot be washed away."

Then one day he heard a noise—tap, tap, tap. A stone-cutter stood there, working with mallet and chisel. He drove the sharp tool into the stone as he cut out blocks for the builders.

The great stone shivered as he felt the blows. "Here is someone who is stronger than I," he cried. "I wish I were that man!"

No sooner had he made his wish than he found that was the man. He was Tawara, the stone-cutter, again. He lived in a little hut. He ate simple food and worked from morning till night; but he was happy. All day long he sang as he worked, and he did not wish again to be mightier than others.

"A little home, sweet sleep, and useful work—what is better than these?" said Tawara, the stone-cutter.

—Japanese Tale

THE GOLDEN FISH

THE KIND-HEARTED FISHERMAN

Long ago, an old man and his wife lived upon an island in the middle of the sea. They were so poor that they were often without food.

One day the man had been fishing for many hours, but without any success. At last he caught a small golden fish, with eyes as bright as diamonds.

"Put me back into the sea, kind man," cried the little fish. "I am so small that I would not make a meal for you."

The old man felt so sorry for the little fish that he threw him back into the sea. As the golden fish swam away he called out, "If ever you need anything, call to me. I will come at once to help you. I will do this because you were kind to me."

The fisherman laughed, for he did not believe that a fish could help him. When he went home, he told his wife what a wonderful fish he had caught.

"What!" she cried. "You put him back into the sea after you had caught him? How foolish you were! We have no food in the house, and now, I suppose, we must starve!"

She scolded him so much that at last the poor man went back to the sea. He did not really believe that the fish would help him, but he thought it would do no harm to find out. "Golden fish, golden fish!" he called. "Come to me, I pray."

As the last word was spoken, the wonderful fish popped his head out of the water.

"I have kept my promise, you see," said the fish. "What can I do for you, my good friend?"

"There is no food in the house," answered the old man, "and my wife is very angry with me for putting you back into the sea."

"Do not be troubled," said the golden fish. "Go home. You will find food, and to spare."

The Fisherman's Wife Learns a Lesson

The old man hurried home to see if his little friend had spoken the truth. He found the oven full of fine white loaves of bread!

"I did not do so badly for you, after all, good wife," said the fisherman, as they ate their supper.

But his wife was not satisfied yet. The more she had, the more she wanted. All that night she lay awake, planning other things to ask of the golden fish.

"Wake up, you lazy man!" she cried to her husband, early in the morning. "Go down to the sea and tell your fish that I must have a new wash-tub."

The old man did as his wife bade him. The moment he called, the fish came, and seemed quite willing to do as he was asked. When the fisherman returned to his home, he saw there a new wash-tub!

"Why didn't you ask for a new house, too?" his wife asked, angrily. "If you had asked for a fine house, he would have given it to us. Go back and say that we must have a new house."

The fisherman did not like to trouble his friend again so soon; but when he went, he found the golden fish as willing to help him as before.

FRANCES KERR COOK

"Very well," said the fish. "A new house you shall have." When the old man went back to his wife, he found a beautiful house instead of his little hut!

It would have pleased him greatly if his wife had been contented now. But she was a foolish woman, and even yet was not satisfied. "Tell your golden fish," she said the next day, "that I want to live in a palace. I want a great many servants to wait upon me, and a splendid carriage to ride in."

Once more her wish was granted. After this, the poor fisherman's life was even more unhappy than before; for his wife would not allow him to share her palace, but made him live in the stable.

"At any rate," he said to himself, "I have peace here." But before long she sent for him again.

"Go down to the sea, and call the golden fish," she commanded. "Tell him I wish to be queen of the Waters and to rule over all the fishes in the sea."

The poor old man thought that he would be sorry for the fishes if she ever ruled over them; for riches had quite spoiled her. Still, he did not dare to disobey her, so once more he called his good friend.

When the golden fish heard what the fisherman's wife wanted this time, he cried out, "Make your wife the queen of the Waters! Never! She is not fit to rule others, for she cannot rule herself. Go home! You will see me no more."

The old man went sorrowfully home, and found the palace changed to a hut. His wife was no longer dressed in rich garments; she was wearing the simple dress of a fisherman's wife. But she was now quiet and mild, and much easier to live with than she had been before.

"After all," thought the fisherman, "I am not sorry that the palace became a hut again."

He worked hard to make a living for himself and his wife, and somehow his hooks were never empty, so that the old couple always had food. Sometimes when he drew in a fish, the sun would gleam upon its scales. Then the old man would think of his little friend who had been so kind to him. But he never saw the golden fish again.

—Russian Tale

BROTHER FOX'S TAR BABY

ACT I

Time—A Hot Summer Day

Place—The Woods

Persons:

Brother Fox   Brother Rabbit

[*Brother Fox is trotting along a path in the woods, and suddenly meets Brother Rabbit.*]

Brother Rabbit. It's a hot day, Brother Fox. Where are you going?

Brother Fox. I'm going fishing. Come along with me.

Brother Rabbit. On a hot day like this? Sit in the sun and fish? No, indeed!

Brother Fox. Well, let's get some boughs and build a little house on the edge of the river. Then we can sit in it and be cool while we fish.

Brother Rabbit. Build a house this hot day? No, thank you! I don't care for fish, anyway. A few green leaves are all I need.

Brother Fox. [*Angrily.*] Very well, then! But I'm going to build a cool little house. It will be my own house, and I shall fish there alone!

BROTHER RABBIT. All right, Brother Fox. Good-bye!

[*Brother Rabbit runs* off *down the path.*]

BROTHER FOX. Now I'll build my house; and I'd like to see Brother Rabbit set his foot in it.

[*Brother Fox goes to the river bank and builds a house of boughs.*]

ACT II

Time—THE NEXT AFTERNOON

Place—BROTHER FOX'S LITTLE HOUSE

Persons:

BROTHER FOX   BROTHER RABBIT

[*Brother Rabbit is sitting in Brother Fox's house, fishing. He hears a sound.*]

BROTHER RABBIT. That must be Brother Fox! I'll run up the bank and hide in the bushes.

[*He hides, and a moment later Brother Fox comes along with a basket and a fish-pole.*]

BROTHER FOX. Now for a fine basket of fish! No more sitting in the hot sun for me! [*Suddenly he sees tracks near the door.*] What are these? Rabbit-tracks? So Brother Rabbit has been in my house! Oh, I wish I could catch him fishing here! But how can I do it? [*After a moment's thought.*] I have it! I have it! Look out, Brother Rabbit! I'll catch you yet!

[*Brother Fox runs of down the path, and Brother Rabbit runs home, laughing.*]

ACT III

Time—THE AFTERNOON OF THE THIRD DAY
Place—THE LITTLE HOUSE BY THE RIVER

Persons:

BROTHER FOX   BROTHER RABBIT
THE TAR BABY

[*Brother Fox steals through the bushes, carrying a wooden doll covered with tar.*]

BROTHER FOX. I'll catch Brother Rabbit this time. How soft and sticky this tar is!

[*Brother Fox puts the Tar Baby on the path near the little house. Then he hides in the bushes. By and by Brother Rabbit comes down the path, with his fish-pole and line.*]

BROTHER RABBIT. [*Looking around.*] No one here! Now for a cool fish! [*Suddenly he sees the Tar Baby.*] Hello, there! Who are you?

[*The Tar Baby says nothing.*]

BROTHER RABBIT. Why don't you answer me?

[*The Tar Baby says nothing.*]

BROTHER RABBIT. [*Going up closer.*] See here!
Have you no tongue in your black head? Answer
me! Speak up in a hurry, or I'll hit you.

[*The Tar Baby says nothing. Brother Rabbit
hits him with his right hand. It sticks fast.*]

BROTHER RABBIT. [*Very angry.*] Here! What's this!
Let go my hand. Let go, I tell you! Will you let
go? [*He raises his left hand.*]

[*The Tar Baby says nothing. Brother Rabbit
strikes—Bam! His left hand sticks fast.*]

BROTHER RABBIT. [*In a rage.*] Turn me loose! [*He
raises his right foot.*] Do you see this foot? Do
you want me to kick you with it?

[*The Tar Baby says nothing. Brother Rabbit kicks him—Bom! His foot sticks fast.   He quickly raises the other.*]

BROTHER RABBIT. [*Shouting.*] Do you think I have only one foot? See this one! If I kick you with it, you'll think it is Brother Bear knocking your teeth out!

[*The Tar Baby says nothing. Brother Rabbit kicks him—Boom! His left foot sticks fast, too. He wags his head back and forth.*]

BROTHER RABBIT. [*Screaming.*] Look out now! Turn me loose! If I butt your woolly head, it will be the last of you. You'll never stop till you strike the bottom of the river. Answer me! Will you turn me loose?

[*The Tar Baby says nothing. Brother Rabbit butts him—Biff! His head sticks fast.*]

BROTHER RABBIT. [*Whining.*] Black boy, let me go! Turn me loose! I was just playing!

BROTHER FOX. [*Running from the bushes and dancing up and down with joy.*] How do you like my Tar Baby, Brother Rabbit? I have you now! You'll see what happens to people who steal into my little house.

BROTHER RABBIT. [*Whining.*] Let me go, Brother Fox! Let me go. I am your friend.

BROTHER FOX. I don't want a thief for a friend. I think I'll just build a big fire.

BROTHER RABBIT. [*Frightened.*] What for, Brother Fox? What for?

BROTHER FOX. I think I'll have a roast for dinner. Roast rabbit is good.

[*Brother Fox gathers branches and puts them down beside Brother Rabbit and the Tar Baby. Then he sets the branches on fire, and goes off for more firewood.*]

BROTHER RABBIT. [*Squirming.*] Oh, oh, my hair and whiskers! I'm scorching! Turn me loose! [*As the fire grows hotter it melts the tar, and one of Brother Rabbit's hands is loosened.*] My hand is loose! Hurrah! This Tar Baby is melting! Hurrah, hurrah! [*He squirms again.*]

BROTHER FOX. [*Returning and throwing on more branches.*] How is that, Brother Rabbit? Is that fire big enough to roast a rabbit?

[*Brother Rabbit stops squirming. He sits very still and does not let Brother Fox see that one of his hands is loose.*]

Brother Rabbit. [*Scornfully.*] Do you call this a fire? You'll have to build a bigger one than this to scare me!

Brother Fox. [*Very angry.*] You shall have fire enough to do more than scare you. I'll bring an armful that will roast you.

[*Brother Fox goes off for more branches. While he is away, the fire melts the tar so that Brother Rabbit shakes himself free.*]

Brother Rabbit. [*Calling back as he runs away.*] Build your fire all you want to, Brother Fox! But you can't have roast rabbit this time! How would you like some melted tar?

[*He goes off into the bushes, laughing.*]

—*Frederick Ortoli—Adapted*

THE BROWNIE OF BLEDNOCK

THE WEE MAN COMES TO TOWN

Did you ever hear how a brownie came to the village of Blednock, and was frightened away again?

Well, it was one summer evening, just when the milking was done and before the children were put to bed. The good people of Blednock were sitting on the doorsteps talking to their neighbors, and the children were playing in the dooryards.

All at once they heard a queer, humming noise. Nearer and nearer it sounded, and everyone turned and looked.

It was no wonder that they stared, for coming up the road was the strangest little creature that anyone had ever seen.

He looked like a wee, wee man; and yet such a strange man! His bright red hair was long, and he had a long red beard. His knees knocked together when he walked, and his arms were so long that his hands almost touched the ground. A strange sight he was!

He was singing something over and over. As he came nearer, they could make out the words:

>"Oh, my name is Aiken-Drum,
>And to do your work I've come.
>A bite to eat, a bed on hay,
>You may give; but nothing pay."

Oh, but I can tell you the people were frightened! The little ones screamed, and the larger girls dropped the pails of milk they were carrying home. The big boys, who should have known better, hooted at the little man.

"Did you ever see such eyes?" cried one.

"Look at his long beard!" said another.

But still the little man went slowly up the street. singing

>"Oh, my name is Aiken-Drum,
>And to do your work I've come.
>A bite to eat, a bed on hay,
>You may give; but nothing pay."

GRANNY DUNCAN'S ADVICE

Granny Duncan was the oldest and kindest woman in the village. Oh, she was very old! She knew all the tales of the olden time.

"I think this is just a harmless brownie," she said. "Long ago I heard of brownies from my father's father. We will take Baby Meg to see him. If she smiles upon him, he is just a brownie. For babies always love brownies and know them when they see them."

So Baby Meg was brought, and she laughed and put out her tiny hands to the strange little man.

"He is just a good, kind brownie!" cried Granny Duncan. "Many a long day's work will he do for people who treat him well."

Then everybody grew very brave, and crowded around him. When they were close to him they saw that his hairy face was kind, and that his big eyes had a merry twinkle in them.

"Can you not speak?" asked an old man. "Tell us where you came from."

"I cannot tell you where I came from," said the wee man. "My country has no name, and it is not at all like this land of yours. For there, we all learn to serve, while here, everyone wishes to be served. We love to work. It sometimes happens that there is no work for us at home. Then one of us may come to your land, to see if you have need of him."

"Do you really like to work?" asked Idle Tom.

"I love to serve," said the brownie. "He serves himself best, who serves others most. If I am needed, I will stay in this place a while. I do not want clothes, or a bed, or wages. All I ask for is a corner of the barn to sleep in, and a bowl of broth at bedtime.

"If no one troubles me, I will be ready to help anyone who needs me. I'll bring in the sheep from the hill. I'll gather the harvest by moonlight. I'll bake your bread on a busy day. I'll sing the babies to sleep in their cradles. The babies always love me."

No one knew what to say. A little man who would do everything for nothing! It could not be true! There must be something wrong about it! Men began to whisper to each other. "Perhaps it would be better to have nothing to do with him," they said.

Then Granny Duncan spoke up again. "He's just a harmless brownie, I tell you," she said. "Have you not all complained about your hard work? Here is a good workman all ready to help you. Will you turn him away just because he looks so queer?"

"But he will frighten our friends," said the young people. "They will not come to the village if we let him stay. Then it will be lonely here."

"Handsome is, as handsome does," said Granny Duncan. "I have heard that a brownie can stack a whole ten-acre field of wheat in a single night."

"A ten-acre field in a single night! Just think of that!" said all the men. So the miller told the brownie that he might sleep in his barn, and Granny Duncan promised him a bowl of broth at bedtime.

Then all said good-night and went home, looking over their shoulders to see if the strange little man was following them. You may be very sure that no one lingered behind, that night.

THE BROWNIE'S GOOD DEEDS

All the people of the village were a little afraid at first, but in a week everyone was praising the brownie. For Aiken-Drum was the most wonderful worker that ever was seen, and the strange thing was that he did nearly all of his work at night.

If there was a tired baby to sing to sleep, or a house to be made tidy, or a churnful of cream that would not turn to butter, or bread that would not rise, Aiken-Drum always knew about it. He would come at just the right time.

He gathered the sheep together on stormy nights. He carried home the heavy bundle for a tired man. He stacked the grain safely.

Many a time some poor mother would be up all night with a sick child. She would sit down in front of the fire and fall fast asleep.

When she awoke she would find that Aiken-Drum had made her a visit. The floor would be scrubbed, the dishes washed, the fire made, and the kettle put on to boil. But the little man would have slipped quietly away, for he never waited to be thanked.

And the village was not lonely, oh, no! People came from everywhere to see if they could catch a glimpse of the strange little visitor.

But they never saw him. One could go to the miller's barn twenty times a day; and twenty times a day one would find nothing but a little heap of hay. The bowl that held his food was always empty in the morning, but no one ever saw the brownie eating the broth.

Little children were the only ones who ever saw him; and oh, how he loved them! Just before bed-time, they would gather around him in some quiet corner by the old mill.

Then the villagers would hear wonderful, low, sweet music. It was Aiken-Drum, singing the songs of his own land to the happy children.

Why Aiken-Drum Left Blednock

And he might be there yet, gathering the harvest and helping tired people with their work; but someone forgot what the little man had said, over and over again, in his strange song

"A bite to eat, a bed on hay,
You may give; but nothing pay."

You see, a brownie loves to give; he will not work for pay. But someone forgot this.

"I must make something for Aiken-Drum," said a poor woman whom he had helped. "He never will stay to let me thank him. Winter is coming on, and he will be cold in his old worn suit. I will make him a warm coat."

So she cut and sewed and pressed and made a little coat for the brownie. She told no one what she was doing; but one night she put the last stitch in the pretty little garment. Then she went softly to the miller's barn and laid it down beside the bowl of broth.

Never again did Aiken-Drum work for the people of Blednock. The strange little man was obliged to go away, for a true brownie cannot stay where he is paid.

But sometimes the children hear his voice down by the old mill. It is always soft and low and sweet. He is singing the songs of his own land, just as he used to do when the little ones were gathered around him.

Then the good people in the village remember his kind deeds and his strange saying, "He serves himself best, who serves others most."

—*Elizabeth W. Grierson*

THE FAIRIES

Up the airy mountain,
  Down the rushy glen,
We daren't go a-hunting
  For fear of little men;
Wee folk, good folk,
  Trooping all together;
Green jacket, red cap,
  And white owl's feather!

Down along the rocky shore
  Some make their home;
They live on crispy pancakes
  Of yellow sea-foam;
Some in the reeds
  Of the black mountain lake,
With frogs for their watchdogs,
  All night awake.

By the craggy hillside,
  Through the mosses bare,
They have planted thorn trees
  For pleasure here and there.
If any man so daring
  As dig them up in spite
He shall find the sharpest thorns
  In his bed at night.

Up the airy mountain,
  Down the rushy glen,
We daren't go a-hunting
  For fear of little men;
Wee folk, good folk,
  Trooping all together;
Green jacket, red cap,
  And white owl's feather!

         —*William Allingham*

HOW DOUGHNUTS CAME TO BE MADE

Once there was a little cook who had eyes as dark as black currants; cheeks as pink as his best frosting; and skin as white as the finest pastry flour.

As for his hair, it was exactly the color of brown sugar, and you know what a pleasing color that is. He wore a snowy cap and apron, and always had a long wooden spoon hanging from his belt.

He was the very best cook that ever lived, for he never cooked anything that was not good. Jam, and little round plum cakes with pink and white frosting; and kisses, and lemon pie, and straw-

berry ice-cream, and little three-cornered raspberry tarts, and oranges cut into baskets and filled
with whipped cream—oh, there was no end to the
good things this little cook would make!

He made spice-cake, too; and what do you think?
One day when he was making spice-cake, he happened to look out of the window and saw, walking
by, a little fairy, as pretty as a pink rose. She was
a cook, too, and she had on a cap and an apron
exactly like his! The little cook ran to the door, and
called out, "Pretty little Fairy, won't you come in?"

The little fairy said, "I thank you, kind sir." Then
she came in and sat down.

The little cook had dinner all ready, and he
brought her some turtle soup, in a little china bowl
all painted with butterflies; three oyster patties,
the best you ever saw; a fat little quail on toast,
with mashed potatoes and gravy; a mince turnover
and a lemon tart; a glass of orange jelly; a saucer
of ice-cream; and some macaroons!

When the little fairy had eaten all these dainties,
the little cook asked her, " Can you cook as well as
I cooked this dinner?"

"Just as well, but no better," answered the fairy.

"Was there anything that could have been cooked better?" he asked.

"Yes; the piece of toast under the quail was darker on one side than on the other," she answered.

"You are right," said the little cook; "but only a wonderful cook would have noticed such a fine point. If we worked together, we could make the most delicious dainties in the world. Will you marry me?"

"That I will, with all my heart," said the little fairy; "but where can we find a preacher?"

Just at that moment, who should come into the room but the village preacher, to buy a three-cornered raspberry tart!

"You shall have the tart for nothing," said the little cook, "if you will marry us."

"I will marry you very gladly," said the preacher. "But where is the wedding ring?"

The little cook turned round and round and round three times, thinking what he could do. For he had no ring, and he did not know where he could get one. But after the third turn, his eyes fell upon the dough that he had been making for the spice-cake. Then he knew what to do.

He made a little ball of dough and patted it flat. Then he took the little fairy's finger and poked it right through the middle of the dough. Last of all he dropped the dough into a pan of hot fat.

When it was done, it was such a beautiful nut-brown color that the little fairy cried out, "Why, it looks just like a *dough* nut!"

As soon as it had cooled, the little cook put it upon the fairy's finger, which, of course, it fitted perfectly. Then the preacher married them. After the wedding was over, they filled the preacher's hat with raspberry tarts, buns, and spice-cake; and that was a very good day for the village preacher.

The little cook and the little fairy lived together happily ever afterwards, both stirring the soup at the same time and never quarreling. They often made beautiful brown doughnuts, with little round holes in them, to remind them of their wedding day.

And that is the way doughnuts came to be made.

—*Laura E. Richards—Adapted*

THE FAIRY SHOES

THE FAIRY'S GIFT

Once upon a time a baby boy was born in a little home in a country far away. There was a fine christening feast, and all the friends came. The baby's mother had a fairy godmother, and of course she was invited, too.

"She is rich," said all the friends. "No doubt she will bring a splendid gift."

But when the fairy came, she brought with her only a little brown-paper parcel. How everyone wondered what was in the parcel!

At last the fairy untied the string and opened it. And what do you think was in it? A small pair of leather shoes, with copper tips!

"This is my gift," the fairy said. "It is not quite so poor as it looks, for these little shoes will never wear out. When they grow too small for this little boy, they will be ready for another, and another, and another. But there is something more wonderful still about them. The little feet that wear them cannot go wrong.

"When you send your little boy to school in these shoes, they will pinch his feet if he loiters by the way. When you send him on an errand, they will remind him to go quickly, and they will see that he always gets home on time."

Years went by, and the little family grew larger, until at last there were nine boys. Eight of them, one after the other, had worn the fairy shoes; but they never wore out.

And just as the fairy godmother had said, the feet in the fairy shoes always went where they were sent and always came back home when it was time. So all the boys had learned to be prompt and obedient.

At last it was Timothy's turn to wear the shoes. He was the youngest of the nine sons, and he had been much petted and spoiled.

He had grown very willful, and his feet were pretty well used to taking their own way. At last he played truant from school so often and was late for dinner so many times that his mother said, "Tim, you must wear the fairy shoes."

So the shoes were blackened, and the copper tips were polished; and one morning Timothy put them on to wear to school.

"I hope you will be a good boy, Tim," said his mother. "You must not loiter or play truant, for if you do, these shoes will pinch you, and you will be sure to be found out."

Tim's mother held him by the right arm while she told him these things, and Tim's left arm and both his legs were already as far away as he could stretch them. He did not give a single thought to what she had said.

Tim Learns a Lesson

It was a May morning, and the sun shone brightly. Tim wanted to loiter on this beautiful morning, when every nook had a flower, and every bush a bird.

Once or twice he stopped to pick flowers; but the shoes pinched his feet, and he ran on. But when the path led near the swamp, and he saw the marsh-marigolds in bloom, he stopped.

"I must have some of these beauties," he said. "They are like cups of gold!" Tim forgot everything that his mother had said and began to scramble down the steep bank to the swamp.

But how strangely his shoes behaved! As often as he turned toward the shining flowers, the fairy shoes turned back again toward school. They pinched and pulled and twisted until Tim feared that his ankles would be broken.

In spite of the fairy shoes, Tim dragged himself down to the swamp. But when he got there, be could not find a flower within reach. All the marigolds were far out in the marsh. The fairy shoes jerked and twisted, but Tim went on and on. At last he got near a great cluster of the golden flowers.

"I will have them!" he said; and he gave a great jump. Down he sank into the swamp. But when he pulled his feet out of the thick black mud, off came the troublesome fairy shoes!

"I'll just leave the fairy shoes in the mud," he said. "That's the way to see the last of them!"

Tim wondered why his brothers had never thought of this good plan. He went on easily now, wading from cluster to cluster, until he had a great handful of the bright marsh-marigolds.

At last, when Tim was beginning to feel tired, he hurt his foot on a sharp stump. Just then a fat green frog jumped so close to his face that it frightened him, and he nearly fell backward into the water.

Out he scrambled, and up the bank he climbed! After cleaning himself as well as he could with his little handkerchief, he went on to school.

"What shall I say to the teacher?" Tim thought. "Oh, how I wish I had done as the fairy shoes wanted me to do!"

The little truant reached the school and quietly opened the door. The boys of his class were standing ready for a lesson. As soon as they saw Tim, all of the children began to laugh.

What do you think had happened? There on the floor, just where Tim should have stood, were the fairy shoes! In each of them was a beautiful marsh-marigold.

"You have been in the swamp, Timothy," said the teacher. "Put on your shoes at once."

When his lessons and his punishment were over, Tim was glad enough to let the fairy shoes take him straight home. After that, he heeded the little shoes and soon learned to be as prompt and obedient as his brothers.

—Juliana Horatio Ewing—Adapted

THE BROWNIES

TOMMY'S DREAM

Wonderful stories grandmother told Johnnie and Tommy—stories of hobgoblins and dwarfs and fairies! Once she told them about a brownie who lived in her own family long ago.

He was a little fellow, no larger than Tommy, she said, but very active. He slept by the fire, and he was so shy that no one ever saw him.

But early in the morning, when all the family were in their beds, this brownie would get up, sweep the room, build the fire, set the table, milk the cow, churn the cream, bring the water, and scrub the floors until there was not a speck of dirt anywhere.

The children liked this story very much, and oh, how they did wish such a brownie would come to live in their house!

Over and over again they asked, "Was there really and truly a brownie, Grandmother? How we wish he would come back again! Why, he could mind the baby, and tidy the room, and bring in the wood, and wait on you, Grandmother! Can't we do something to get him back again?"

"I don't know, my dears," said Grandmother. "But when I was a young girl, they used to say that if one set a bowl of bread and milk, or even a pan of clear water for him overnight, he would be sure to come. And just for that, he would do all the work."

"Oh! let us try it!" said both the boys; and Johnnie ran to get a pan, while Tommy brought fresh water from the well. They knew, poor hungry lads, that there was no bread or milk in the house. Their father, who was a poor tailor, could hardly earn money enough to buy food for them all. His wife was dead, and the work of the house took so much of his time that he could not make many coats.

Johnnie and Tommy were idle and lazy. They were too thoughtless to help their father, although they were strong young boys.

One night, soon after this, Tommy had a wonderful dream. He thought he went down to the meadow by the old mill pond. There he saw an owl, that rolled its great eyes, and called out, "Tu-whit, tuwhoo! Tommy, what are you doing way down here at this time of night?"

"Please, I came to find the brownies," said Tommy; "can you tell me where they live?"

"Tu-whoo, tu-whoo !" screamed the old owl; "so it's the brownies you are after, is it? Tu-whoo, tu-whoo! Go look in the mill pond. Tu-whoo, tu-whoo! Go look in the water at midnight, and you'll see one. By the light of the moon, a brownie you'll see, to be sure, but such a lazy one! Tu-whoo, tu-whoo!" screamed the old owl, as it flew away.

"The mill pond, at midnight, by moonlight!" thought Tommy. What could the old owl mean? It was midnight then, and moonlight, too; and there he was, right down by the water. "Silly old thing," said Tommy; "brownies don't live in the water."

But for all that, Tommy went to the bank of the pond and peeped in. The moon was shining as bright as day; and what do you suppose Tommy saw? Why just a picture of himself in the water! That was all.

"I am not a brownie!" he said to himself. But the longer he looked, the harder he thought.

At last he said to himself, "I wonder if I am a brownie! Perhaps I am one, after all. Grandmother said they are about as large as I am. And the owl said I would see a very lazy one if I looked in the water. Am I lazy? That must be what the old owl meant. I am the brownie myself!"

The longer he thought about it, the surer he was
that he must be a brownie. "Why," he thought, "if
I am one, Johnnie must be another; then there are
two of us. I'll go home and tell Johnnie about it."

Off he ran as fast as his legs could carry him,
and just as he was calling, "Johnnie, Johnnie! We
are brownies! The old owl told me!" he found himself wide awake, sitting up in bed, and rubbing his
eyes while Johnnie lay fast asleep by his side.

The first faint rays of morning light were just.
creeping in through the bedroom window. "Johnnie, Johnnie, Johnnie, wake up!" cried Tommy. "I
have: something to tell you!"

After he had told his brother all about his
strange dream, Tommy said, "Let us play that we
really are brownies, Johnnie, even if we are not.
Let us do the housework and be like the brownies
that grandmother told us about. It will be great
fun to surprise Father and Grandmother. We will
keep out of sight and tell about it afterwards. Oh,
do come! It will be such fun!"

So these two brownies put on their clothes in a
great hurry and crept softly to the kitchen. There
they found enough work for a dozen brownies to do.

The Brownies at Work

Tommy built a fire, and while the kettle was boiling, swept the untidy floor. Johnnie dusted his grandmother's chair, made the cradle ready for his baby sister, and set the table for breakfast.

Just as they had finished their work, they heard their father's footstep on the stairs. "Run!" whispered Tommy, "or father will see us." So away the boys scampered to their room.

How surprised the poor tailor was when he saw the work that had been done in the kitchen! He thought that the brownies he had heard about in his childhood had come back again.

The old grandmother was much pleased. "What did I tell you?" she said. "I have always known that there are real brownies."

Although it was fun for the boys to play that they were brownies, it was hard work, too. They sometimes thought they would stop playing brownie, but then they would think of their hard-working father and would grow quite ashamed.

Now, things were much better at home than they had been before. The tailor never scolded; Grandmother was more cheerful; the baby was less fretful; and the house was always tidy.

The tailor had more time for his work, now that the brownies helped to keep the house in order. He could make more coats and could get more money. There was always bread and milk enough for everyone, and each night the boys set out on the doorstep a great bowlful for the brownie's supper.

At last the tailor said, "I am going to do something for that brownie. He has done so much for all of us." So he cut and stitched the neatest little coat you ever saw. "I have always heard," he said, "that a brownie's clothes are ragged, and so I know that our brownie will need this."

When the coat was finished, it was very beautiful, all stitched with gold thread and covered with brass buttons. The strangest thing about it was that it just fitted Tommy.

That night the little coat was placed by the bowl of milk set for the brownie. At daybreak, the tailor was awakened by the sound of laughter and scuffling in the kitchen. "That must be the brownie," he thought; and getting out of bed he crept softly down the stairs.

But when he reached the kitchen, instead of the brownie, he saw Johnny and Tommy sweeping and making the fire and dusting and setting the table.

Tommy had put on the coat that his father had made for the brownie and was skipping about in it. He was laughing and calling to Johnnie to see how fine he looked in it. "Johnnie," he said, "I wish father had made it to fit you."

"Boys, what does all this mean?" cried the surprised tailor. "Tommy, why have you put on that coat?"

When the boys saw their father, they ran to him and said, "There is no brownie, Father! We have done the work. And, oh, Father! we are sorry that we were lazy and idle so long; but we mean to be brownies now, real brownies; and help you till we grow to be big men."

The poor tailor was so happy that there were tears in his eyes as he kissed his boys.

Tommy and Johnnie kept their promise. But after a while, their little sister grew to be the best brownie of all. She kept her father's house bright and clean with brush and broom and dustpan.

—Jane L. Hoxie—Adapted

THE JUMBLIES

They went to sea in a sieve, they did;
   In a sieve they went to sea;
In spite of all their friends could say,
On a winter's morn, on a stormy day,
   In a sieve they went to sea.
Far and few, far and few,
   Are the lands where the Jumblies live;
Their heads are green, and their hands are blue
   And they went to sea in a sieve.

They sailed away in a sieve, they did,
   In a sieve they sailed so fast,
With only a beautiful pea-green veil
Tied with a ribbon, by way of a sail,
   To a small tobacco-pipe mast.
And everyone said who saw them go,
   "Oh! won't they be soon upset, you know?
For the sky is dark, and the voyage is long;
And, happen what may, it's extremely wrong
   In a sieve to sail so fast."

They sailed to the Western Sea, they did—
   To a land all covered with trees;
And they bought an owl, and a useful cart,
And a pound of rice, and a cranberry-tart,
   And a hive of silvery bees;
And they bought a pig, and some green jackdaws,
And a lovely monkey with lollipop paws,
And forty bottles of ring-bo-ree,
   And no end of Stilton cheese.

And in twenty years they all came back—
   In twenty years or more;
And everyone said, "How tall they've grown!
For they've been to the Lakes, and the Torrible
   Zone,
   And the hills of the Chankly Bore."
And they drank their health, and gave them a feast
Of dumplings made of beautiful yeast;
And everyone said, "If we only live,
We, too, will go to sea in a sieve,
   To the hills of the Chankly Bore."
Far and few, far and few,
   Are the lands where the Jumblies live;
Their heads are green, and their hands are blue
   And they went to sea in a sieve.

                    —*Edward Lear*

THE SKYLARK'S SPURS

THE UNKIND FAIRY

There was once a fairy who had one very bad habit. She liked to find fault with everybody.

One day when she lay down in a meadow to take a nap, she heard a deep sigh. Peeping out, she saw a young skylark sitting near her in the grass.

"What troubles you?" asked the fairy.

"Oh, I am so unhappy," replied the poor lark; "I want to build a nest, but I have no mate."

"Why don't you look for a mate, then?" said the fairy, laughing at him. "Do you expect one to come and look for you? Fly up into the sky and sing a beautiful song, and then perhaps some pretty bird will hear you. If you tell her that you will help her to build a nest, and that you will sing to her all day long, maybe she will become your mate."

"Oh, I don't like to fly up," said the lark; "I am so ugly. If I were a robin, with red feathers on my breast, I should not mind showing my feet. But I am only a poor skylark, and I know that I shall never be able to get a mate."

"But you should try, anyway," said the fairy.

"Oh, but you don't know," said the lark, "that if I fly up, my feet will be seen; and no other bird has claws like mine. They are so long that they would frighten anyone. And yet, Fairy, I never harm anyone with my long claws."

"Let me look at them," said the fairy.

The lark lifted up one of his feet, which he had kept hidden in the long grass.

"Are you sure that you never use your claws to fight with?" asked the fairy.

"I never fought in my life," said the lark; "yet these claws grow longer and longer."

"Well, I am sorry for you," said the fairy; "but I think that you must be a quarrelsome bird, or you would not have such long spurs."

"That is just what I am always afraid people will say," said the poor lark.

"Well, nothing is given to us unless it is to be of some use," said the fairy. "You would not have wings unless you used them for flying. So you would not have spurs unless you used them for fighting."

"I am sure I never fight," said the lark. "So I thought you might be willing to say to your friends that I am not a quarrelsome bird."

"No," said the unkind fairy, "I still think those spurs are meant to fight with. Good morning."

THE SKYLARK WINS A MATE

After the fairy had left, the poor lark sat quietly in the grass for a long time. By and by a grasshopper came chirping up and tried to comfort him.

"I heard what the unkind fairy said to you. But I have known you a long time, and I have never seen you fight. I will tell everyone that you are a very good-tempered bird."

The skylark was so pleased at these kind words that he flew up into the air. The higher he went, the sweeter was the song that he sang.

"I never heard such a beautiful song in my life—never!" cried a pretty brown lark.

"It was sung by my friend, the skylark," said the grasshopper. "He is a very good-tempered bird, and he wants a mate."

"Hush!" said the pretty brown lark. "I want to hear the end of that wonderful song." She held her breath while she listened.

"Well done, my friend!" said the grasshopper when the skylark came down again. Then he told him how much the brown lark had been pleased with his song. A moment later, he took the poor skylark to see her.

The skylark thought that never before had he seen such a pretty bird. "I hope she will not be afraid of my long spurs," he said to himself.

When she told him how much she loved music, he sprang up again into the blue sky and sang even more sweetly than before. How happy he was to think that he could please her!

The grasshopper began to praise the singer, and to say what a kind, cheerful bird he was. And so after a while, when the skylark asked the brown lark to become his mate, she made his heart glad by saying, "Yes."

"I do not mind your spurs," she said. "I should not like you to have short claws like other birds, although I cannot say exactly why, for they do not seem to be of any use."

What the Skylark's Spurs Were For

After a time, the skylark and the brown lark built a little nest in the grass. The skylark was so happy that he almost forgot about his long spurs.

But the unkind fairy did not forget about them. One afternoon she happened to see the lark's friend. "How do you do, Grasshopper?" she asked.

"Thank you, I am very well and very happy," answered the grasshopper. "People are so kind to me."

"How is your quarrelsome friend, the lark?" asked the fairy.

"He is not quarrelsome," replied the grasshopper "and I wish you would not say that he is."

"Oh, well," said the fairy, laughing, "the lark does not wear those long spurs for nothing."

The grasshopper did not argue with the fairy, but said, "Suppose you come and see the eggs that the pretty brown lark has in her nest."

Off they went together; but what was their surprise to find the little lark trembling and weeping as she sat upon the nest.

"Oh, my pretty eggs!" said the lark when she saw her visitors. "They will certainly be broken."

What is the matter?" asked the grasshopper. "Dear Grasshopper," said the lark, "I have just heard the farmer say that tomorrow morning he will begin to cut the grass in this meadow."

"It is a great pity," said the grasshopper, "that you laid your eggs on the ground!"

"Larks always do," said the little bird, weeping. Neither the grasshopper nor the fairy could do anything to help her.

At last her mate, the skylark, dropped down from the white cloud where he had been singing. In great fright, he asked what the matter was. When they told him, he was very sad, but after a while he lifted his feet and began to look at his long spurs.

"If I had only laid my eggs on the other side of the hedge," cried the poor little brown lark, "they would be safe now."

"My dear," said the skylark, "don't be unhappy." As he said these words, he hopped to the nest, laid the claws of one foot upon the prettiest egg, and clasped it with his long spur. And what do you think he found? The spur exactly fitted the little egg!

"Oh, my good mate!" cried the mother bird; "do you think that you can carry all the eggs to a safe place?"

"To be sure I can," replied the skylark, beginning slowly and carefully to hop, with the egg in his right foot. "I have always wondered what my spur could be for, and now I see."

So he hopped along with the egg, until he came to a safe place on the other side of the hedge. There he put it down and came back for the others.

"Hurrah!" cried the grasshopper. "Lark's spurs forever!"

The fairy did not have a word to say. She felt very much ashamed of herself, because she had told the skylark that his spurs were meant to fight with. She sat looking on in silence, until the last of the eggs had been carried to the other side of the hedge.

Then the skylark sprang up into the sky again, singing to his proud little mate. He was very happy, because now he knew what his long spurs were for.

—Jean Ingelow— Adapted

FAREWELL TO THE FARM

The coach is at the door at last;
The eager children, mounting fast
And kissing hands, in chorus sing:
Good-bye, good-bye, to everything!

To house and garden, field and lawn,
The meadow-gates we swung upon,
To pump and stable, tree and swing,
Good-bye, good-bye, to everything!

And fare you well for evermore,
O ladder at the hayloft door,
O hayloft where the cobwebs cling,
Good-bye, good-bye, to everything!

Crack goes the whip, and off we go;
The trees and houses smaller grow;
Last, round the woody turn we swing;
Good-bye, good-bye, to everything!

—*Robert Louis Stevenson*

A GOOD PLAY

We built a ship upon the stairs
All made of the back-bedroom chairs,
And filled it full of sofa pillows
To go a-sailing on the billows.

We took a saw and several nails,
And water in the nursery pails;
And Tom said, "Let us also take
An apple and a slice of cake";
Which was enough for Tom and me
To go a-sailing on, till tea.

We sailed along for days and days,
And had the very best of plays;
But Tom fell out and hurt his knee,
So there was no one left but me.

—*Robert Louis Stevenson*

THE PRINCESS WHO NEVER LAUGHED

The Little Old Man

There was once a wood-cutter who had three sons. He was very proud of the two older boys, but he thought the youngest son was a simpleton.

One day the oldest son started out to cut wood in the forest. His mother gave him some fine, brown pancakes to take with him for his lunch. He had not gone very far when he met a little old man who said, "Good morning, friend! I see you have plenty of food there. Will you give me a little?"

"Not I," replied the oldest son. "I might not have enough for myself." So he went on, leaving the little man by the roadside. Soon he began his work, but at the very first stroke, his ax cut his arm.

The next day the second son started out to cut wood, and his mother gave him a nice cake to take with him. In the forest he met the same little old man, who begged for a piece of cake.

"No!" cried the second son. "I might not have enough for myself." So he turned away and began to chop at a tree. The very next moment he struck his leg such a blow that he shouted with pain.

In the morning the youngest son went to his father and said, "There is no wood for our fire, and both my brothers have cut themselves. Let me take an ax and see what I can do."

"You!" cried his father. "You do not understand wood-cutting."

"Let me try," said the boy so eagerly that at last his father told him that he might go. His mother made him a little, plain cake, and off he started.

In the forest he met the same little man, who said, "I am very hungry. Please give me some cake."

"Gladly," replied the boy. "The cake is very plain, but you are welcome to a share of it." Then they sat down together, and what was the boy's surprise to find that the cake in his basket was a rich one!

When they had eaten it, the little man said, "You are kind-hearted and shall have your reward. Cut down that tree, and at the roots you will find something worth having."

Then the little man disappeared. The boy took his ax and cut down the tree. At the roots he found a goose with feathers of pure gold! Taking it under his arm, he went to an inn for the night.

Why the Princess Laughed

Now the inn-keeper had three daughters, and when they saw the golden goose, they wanted it.

In the middle of the night, the oldest daughter got out of bed and crept to the room where the boy had left the goose. She said to herself, "At least I will have one golden feather." But no sooner had she touched the goose than her finger and thumb stuck fast, and she could not get them away.

Soon the second daughter came to the room, and, seeing her sister, cried out, "You greedy girl! You want all the feathers for yourself!" But when she tried to pull her away from the goose, her fingers stuck fast to her sister, and she could not get them away.

Then the third daughter came into the room, and saw her two sisters there. She was very angry, for she had intended to take some of the golden feathers, herself. So she took hold of her second sister, and at once found herself a prisoner. In this position the three sisters were obliged to stay for the rest of the night.

Early in the morning the boy put the goose under his arm and set out for home. The three daughters of the inn-keeper were obliged to follow, because their hands were stuck fast.

They had not gone far when they met two lads, who called to the boy, "Stop! Set those girls free!" As he made no answer, they took hold of the sisters to pull them away. But their hands stuck fast, too, and they were obliged to follow.

Many others whom they met tried to help them. But all found themselves stuck fast! At last there was a long line of men and women following the golden goose—all stuck together as if they had been glued. It was the most amusing sight that anyone had ever seen.

In this way they came to a large town, where there lived the richest king in the world. Now this king had a daughter who was so unhappy that no one had ever been able to make her laugh. All day long she sat at her window, looking out sadly.

At last her father became so troubled about her that he cried out, "Whoever is able to make the princess laugh shall have her for his wife!"

It so happened that the princess was at her window when the boy came down the street with the golden goose. When she saw the long line of

people walking after him and trying to break loose, she laughed until the tears ran down her cheeks.

At once her maid rushed to the king to tell him the news. The king was so pleased that he sent out his servants to bring the boy before him. In he came, with his precious goose under his arm, and the wedding was held soon afterwards.

In this strange way the wood-cutter's youngest son became a great prince, and lived in wealth and happiness for the rest of his life.

—*Peter Christen Asbjörnsen*

THE BOY AND HIS CAP

I know a boy whose eyes are bright,
And sharper than a cat's at night;
He never even has to squint
When looking at the finest print.

A thousand things he's sure to spy,
Things that escape his mother's eye;
But though his bright eyes fairly snap,
He never, somehow, sees his cap.

I've seen him hunt it everywhere,
On every table, every chair,
And when his strength was wasted, quite,
His mother saw it, plain in sight.

I wonder if some fellow here
Can make this funny thing quite clear—
Can tell me why a bright-eyed chap,
Can never, never find his cap.

—*Rebecca B. Foresman*

THE GOLDEN PEARS

THE FIRST BASKET OF PEARS

There was once a poor man who had nothing in the world but three sons and a fine pear tree which grew in front of his cottage.

Now the king of that country was very fond of pears. So one day the man said to his sons, "1 shall send the king, as a present, a basketful of our golden pears."

Then he gathered the finest pears from the tree, large ones as yellow as gold, and laid them in a basket. "Take these to the king," he said to his oldest son. "Be sure that you do not let anyone rob you of them on the way."

"I know how to take care of myself, Father," said the boy. Then he covered the pears with fresh leaves and set out for the king's palace.

After a time, the boy came to a fountain, where he stopped to drink. A little old woman was washing some rags at the fountain and singing a queer little song.

"A witch!" said the boy to himself. "She'll try to get my pears, but I'll be too clever for her."

"A fair day, my lad," said the little old woman. "That's a heavy load you have to carry. What is in your basket?"

"A load of sweepings from the road, to see whether I can make a penny by selling it," he answered.

"Road-sweepings!" repeated the old woman. "You don't mean that?"

"Yes, I do mean it," answered the boy.

"Oh, very well. You will find out when you get to your journey's end," said the old woman, and she went on washing and singing.

"She means something by those words, that's clear," thought the boy. "But there's no harm done, for I haven't let her even look at the pears." So on he went until he came to the palace. When he had told his errand, he was led before the king.

"You have brought me some pears, have you, my boy?" said the king, smiling.

"Yes, Your Majesty, here are some of the finest yellow pears in the world," said the boy.

The king was so pleased to hear this that he began to take off the covering of leaves. But what was his anger to find under it nothing but sweepings from the road! The servants who stood by, at once took the boy off to prison.

"It is all a trick of that old woman by the fountain," he said to himself; "I thought she meant mischief to me."

The Second Basket of Pears

After a time, the father said to his other sons, "You see how well your older brother has fared. He carried the juicy fruit in safety to the king. No doubt the king was so well pleased with the pears that he has kept your brother near him, and has made him a rich man."

"I am as wise as he," said the second brother; "give me a basket of the pears, Father, and let me take it to the king. Then I shall become a rich man, too, but I won't keep my riches all to myself. I will send for you to share them with me."

"Well said, my son," answered the father. And as the pears were just ripe again, he took another basket and filled it with the beautiful yellow fruit.

The second son took the basket and went on his way until he came to the same fountain that his older brother had seen. Here he, too, stopped to get a drink.

The same old woman was washing her rags at the fountain and singing her queer little song.

"A fair day, my lad," she said. "That's a heavy load you have to carry. What is in your basket?"

"It's pigs' food," answered the boy. "I am taking it to market to see whether I can make a penny by selling it."

"Pigs' food!" repeated the little old woman. "You don't mean that?"

"Yes, I do mean it," he answered, rudely.

"Oh, very well; you will find out when you get to your journey's end," she said to him, just as she had said to his brother.

The boy went on until he reached the palace. He too, was led before the king with his basket. But when the king uncovered it, there was a basket of pigs' food instead of beautiful yellow pears! The servants took the second boy off to prison, where his brother had been kept so long.

The Third Basket of Pears

As the days went by, and the poor man heard nothing from his two sons, he grew very sad. When the youngest boy saw his father's sorrow, he, too felt sad. So one day he asked whether he might not go in search of his brothers.

"Do you really think that you can find them?" asked the father, who had always thought that his youngest son was a simpleton.

"I do not know, Father, but I will do whatever you tell me to do," replied the boy.

The pears were just ripe again, so the man laid the finest of the yellow fruit in a basket, and sent the youngest son on his way.

As the boy walked along, the day grew very hot. Soon he reached the same fountain that his brothers had seen. There he stopped to drink and to rest.

The same old woman was washing her rags, and singing a queer little song. "Here comes another of those rude boys!" she thought, when she saw the youngest son. "I suppose he, too, will try to fool me. As if I didn't know how sweet is the smell of fine ripe pears!"

"Good morning!" said the boy, taking off his cap politely.

"He has better manners than the other two," thought the little old woman, as she returned his greeting.

"May I sit down here, please?" asked the boy.

"Yes," she answered, greatly surprised by his politeness. "And what have you in your basket, my boy? It must be a very precious load to be worth carrying on such a hot day as this."

"Indeed it is precious," said the boy. "These are ripe, yellow pears, and my father says there are no finer in the whole world. I am taking them to the king, who is very fond of the fruit."

"Only ripe pears, and yet so heavy!" said the old woman, as she lifted the basket. "Your load seems too heavy to be pears. But you will see when you come to your journey's end."

"They are nothing but pears," said the boy politely, as he started on his way again.

How the servants at the palace laughed when another boy came to them with the story that he had pears for the king! "No, no!" they said. "We have had enough of that! You may turn around and go back home."

The poor boy began to weep bitterly. At that moment the king and his little daughter came out of the palace. When the girl saw the weeping boy, she asked what troubled him.

"It is another boy who has come to insult the king," answered the servants. "Your Majesty, shall we take him away to prison?"

"You may decide, Daughter," said the king.

"But I *have* pears!" cried the boy. "And my father says there are no finer in the world."

"We know that story by heart!" cried a servant

"Please look at my pears, fair princess!" pleaded the boy. "I have brought them a long way for the king."

The princess decided to look into the basket, herself. She peeped under the leaves—and there were shining pears of solid gold!

"These *are* pears fit for a king!" she said, as she gave them to her father. The king was so pleased that he ordered the gold fruit to be placed among his treasures. And as a reward for the gift, he promised the boy whatever he might ask.

"All I wish is to find my two brothers, who also brought some pears to Your Majesty," said the boy.

"Those other boys who said they brought pears, are now in prison," said the king. Then he commanded that they be brought before him. As soon as the two brothers were led in, the youngest boy ran to them and kissed them.

When the two older boys had told how they came to be thrown into prison, the king said, "It is always best to tell the truth." The boys had often heard their father say the same thing, and they were sorry that they had forgotten this when they talked to the old woman at the fountain.

Then the king sent for the father and gave him charge of the gardens about the palace. The happy man brought with him the pear tree that had brought golden fortune to them. And ever after, he and his sons lived in plenty.

—*Angela M. Keyes*

ONLY ONE MOTHER

Hundreds of stars in the pretty sky;
   Hundreds of shells on the shore together;
Hundreds of birds that go singing by;
   Hundreds of bees in the sunny weather.

Hundreds of dewdrops to greet the dawn;
   Hundreds of lambs in the purple clover;
Hundreds of butterflies on the lawn;
   But only one mother the wide world over.

—*George Cooper*

WHICH LOVED BEST?

"I love you, Mother," said little John.
Then forgetting his work, his cap went on,
And he was off to the garden swing,
Leaving his mother the wood to bring.

"I love you, Mother," said little Nell,
"I love you better than tongue can tell."
Then she teased and pouted half the day,
Till mother rejoiced when she went to play.

"I love you, Mother," said little Fan.
"Today I'll help you all I can."
To the cradle then she did softly creep,
And rocked the baby till it fell asleep.

Then stepping softly, she took the broom,
And swept the floor and dusted the room;
Busy and happy all day was she,
Helpful and cheerful as child could be.

"I love you, Mother," again they said—
Three little children, going to bed.
How do you think that mother guessed
Which of them really loved her best?

—Joy Allison

IRENE, THE IDLE

THE FAIRY HOUSE

"Oh, what a pretty little house!" So said Irene, she stood with her fairy godmother outside the fairy cottage.

"Do you think it pretty, Irene? I am glad of that, for it is here you are going to stay."

"That will be lovely! Am I to be all alone?"

"Yes," answered the fairy. "I am going to leave you here to take care of the house. Come inside, and I will tell you what you must do each day."

Leading Irene into a dainty little bedroom, the fairy said to her, "Every morning you must open the windows wide to let in the air. Then you must make the bed and dust the room well.

"This is the parlor," said the fairy, opening a door. "Every day you must sweep the floor and polish the table and the chairs. And this is the kitchen," she said, as she led the way into another room. Then she gave her this advice:

"Be up with the sun, get your work done;

Keep the stove bright and fire alight.

Here are the brushes, here are the brooms;

Here are the dusters for dusting the rooms.

"Now I must leave you. Do your work well, and soon I shall come to see you again. Good-bye, Irene." Then the fairy walked away.

From parlor to bedroom, from bedroom to kitchen, and from kitchen to garden, Irene wandered. Every minute she grew more pleased.

"It is perfectly lovely!" said the happy little girl, in great delight as she looked about her.

Suddenly she heard a voice call out, "Now, then, little mistress, if you do not give me some wood at once, I shall go out."

Irene nearly jumped out of her shoes. It was—but how could it be?—the fire talking! Speechless with wonder, she sat and stared.

"Very well, then," cried the voice, again; "since you will not take care of me, I shall go out." And, whiff! out went the fire.

Irene went quickly to the wood-box and opened it. Taking some kindling she hurried to the stove.

"Here, mistress, come back and put down my cover, please," called out another voice.

"Now the wood-box is talking," thought Irene. "What a wonderful place this is!"

Then a stick of wood said, "You let me fall, mistress; kindly pick me up."

Irene did as she was told. She closed the wood-box, picked up the wood, and swept the floor. Then she laid the broom upon the table and started to build the fire, when—

"Hang me up, mistress; hang me up in my place," called out the broom.

"I can't do everything at once," said Irene, crossly, as she hung up the broom on its hook.

"One thing at a time, mistress, and each in its proper order," answered the broom.

Soon the fire was burning brightly again. So Irene went to a drawer and got a tablecloth. Then she set the table for dinner.

"Mistress, you have not shut me," called out the drawer, in a loud voice.

"Oh, bother!" cried Irene, as she slammed the drawer in so hard that she knocked down a cup.

"Mistress, hang me up, hang me up!" cried the cup in a shrill voice.

"Oh, stay there and be quiet," she replied, angrily; and the cup said, "Very well, mistress."

"That's better," thought Irene. "If they will only be quiet, I can do things when I have time."

In the pantry she found a little pie, white bread and butter, ripe strawberries, and sweet cream. You may be sure she enjoyed her dinner.

Whenever anything called to her, she answered, "Be quiet; I will attend to you presently," and she was obeyed. After she had finished eating, she piled up the dishes.

"I can wash them by and by," she thought. But as she turned away, the dishes cried, "Mistress, mistress, wash us, wash us, please!"

"Presently," said Irene. "Presently I will."

"Very well, mistress," answered the dishes, just as the cup had done.

Irene sat down to rest. How delightful it was, sitting there! Not a sound was to be heard except the tick of the clock, as it said:

> "The moments fly, one by one,
> Tick, tick!
> Lazy, lazy, nothing done,
> Tick, tick!
> Little moments make the day—
> Swift they come, swift pass away;
> Take them, use them, don't delay,
> Tick, tick, tick, tick!"

THE FAIRY'S WARNING

Irene sat at tea. Everything seemed to be out of place; the hearth was untidy, and the floor unswept. The whole house looked very different frôm the way it had looked when she first came into it.

Suddenly Irene glanced up and saw her fairy godmother standing before her.

"How is this?" demanded the fairy, sternly, as she looked at the untidy room.

"I left things so that I could do them all at once," stammered Irene, very much ashamed.

"Left them to do all at once! You can do only one thing at a time, whenever you begin. Did they not ask to be done?"

"We did, we did!" all the things shouted together; but she told us to be quiet."

"So you want to do them all at once, idle girl? Have your wish. You shall struggle with all these undone tasks, until all of them have been finished." So saying, the fairy disappeared.

Suddenly shouts arose on all sides, "Hang me up!" "Put me away!" "Wash me!" "Sweep me!" All her tasks came crowding about her.

Poor Irene did not know which way to turn. The broom beat her, the cups flew at her head, the table and chairs pushed against her.

At last when the broom gave her a harder blow than before, she seized it and put it on its hook. The broom called out, in a contented voice, "Thank you, mistress."

Irene saw that she must put each thing where it belonged. A dust cloth was striking her in the face. Snatching it up, she dusted the table. Then she folded it and laid it in its place.

"Thank you, mistress," said the duster and the table. So two more things were put in order. Now Irene set to work in earnest, and as each task was completed, she heard the words, "Thank you, mistress." Never before had she worked so hard. She kept on until the little house looked as dainty and clean as it had looked when she came into it.

"Oh, dear!" sighed Irene. "I don't want another evening like this as long as I live."

"Then don't have one, Irene!" ticked the clock. "Don't have one! Do each task as it comes, and then you will find that things will go more pleasantly, and you will have less trouble."

Thank you very much for your advice, Clock," answered Irene. "It sounds strange to hear you and the table and the chairs talk, as you have been doing. I suppose it is because you are all fairy furniture, in a fairy house."

"I suppose so," ticked the clock.

"Well, I am tired, and I think I will go to bed now," said Irene.

"Wind me up first, mistress," cried the clock.

"Oh, yes, I forgot," said Irene; and she wound the clock.

"Mistress, please lock me," said the door.

"And lock me, too," cried the window.

Irene obeyed. Then she took a candle and started to go upstairs. As she did so, she heard the pattering of many little feet.

When she turned around, Irene saw some of the strangest little people in the world. They came jumping out of the clock! Such tiny men they were, each with a long white beard.

Down they scrambled and stood in a circle around the room. Then one of them said, in a shrill voice, "Well, brothers, what do you think of our new mistress?"

"Not very much," answered one of his companions.

"And why not?" asked the first little man.

"She does not know how to make use of us," answered all the other little men, together.

"Then let us teach her how she ought to use us," said the little man. So they all began to sing:

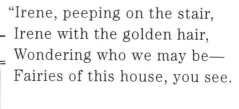

"Irene, peeping on the stair,
Irene with the golden hair,
Wondering who we may be—
Fairies of this house, you see.

"We are minutes of the day,
That so swiftly fly away;
One by one we come to you
With some little task to do.

"You must catch us ere we fly—
You can do it if you try;
Happy then the day will be,
And no trouble you shall see.

"Now to bed and go to sleep;
We a faithful watch will keep,
Waken you when shines the sun,
And the cock crows, 'Night is done.'"

A Happy Birthday

The next morning the warm sunlight streamed in through the window and awoke Irene.

"Ah!" she said to herself, lazily, "I think I will sleep just another half-hour."

"Ding-dong, ding-dong, mistress, get up!" sang the clock from downstairs.

Then Irene remembered all that had happened the day before. "I don't want another day like that," she said, with a shudder.

So she sprang out of bed and dressed herself. After that she opened the windows wide and shook the bed. Then she went downstairs and set to work. When the fairy godmother returned, the cottage was as neat as could be.

"Ah!" cried the fairy, "this is as it should be. How have you managed it, Irene?"

"Sit down, Godmother, and I will tell you. I have done just one thing at a time," answered the happy little girl.

"And so you have found time to do them all. You have learned one lesson, Irene. When you have learned a few more lessons, I shall send you home. For I need my cottage so that I may teach other little girls how to overcome idleness. Now hold up your hand."

Irene obeyed, and her godmother placed a strange looking ring upon her finger. "Every time you are idle, this ring will prick you," said the fairy. "When you have not been pricked once for a whole week, I shall know that you are cured of your idleness."

You must not suppose that Irene found it easy work. Many times the wonderful ring pricked her finger and reminded her of things to be done. But she had made up her mind to try, and it was surprising how quickly she overcame her idleness.

One day, Irene sat at her window, thinking. It was her birthday, and, for the first time, a week had gone by in which the ring had not pricked her once. Suddenly she saw her fairy godmother standing before her,

"Oh, Godmother," cried the happy little girl, "have you, come to give me a birthday party?"

"Yes. That is the very reason I have come, Irene," replied the fairy. "You have learned your lesson well, and I am greatly pleased. Now tell me, are you not much happier than you used to be when you were so idle?"

"Oh, yes, dear Godmother!" answered Irene. "And I have you to thank for it. Now take back your ring, and with it teach some other little girl the lesson I have learned."

—H. Escot-Inman

SUPPOSE

Suppose, my little lady,
  Your doll should break her head,
Could you make it whole by crying
  Till your eyes and nose were red?
And wouldn't it be pleasanter
  To treat it as a joke;
And say you're glad 'twas Dolly's
  And not your head that broke?

Suppose you're dressed for walking,
  And the rain comes pouring down,
Will it clear off any sooner
  Because you scold and frown?
And wouldn't it be nicer
  For you to smile than pout,
And so make sunshine in the house
  When there is none without?

Suppose your task, my little man,
 Is very hard to get,
Will it make it any easier
 For you to sit and fret?
And wouldn't it be wiser,
 Than waiting like a dunce,
To go to work in earnest
 And learn the thing at once?

Suppose that some boys have a horse,
 And some a coach and pair,
Will it tire you less, while walking,
 To say, "It isn't fair"?
And wouldn't it be nobler
 To keep your temper sweet,
And in your heart be thankful
 You can walk upon your feet?

And suppose the world can't please you,
 Nor the way some people do,
Do you think the whole creation
 Will be altered just for you?
And isn't it, my boy or girl,
 The wisest, bravest plan,
Whatever comes, or doesn't come,
 To do the best you can?

      —Phoebe Cary

FRANCES KERR COOK

GOOD-NIGHT AND GOOD-MORNING

A fair little girl sat under a tree,
Sewing as long as her eyes could see;
Then smoothed her work, and folded it right,
And said, "Dear work, good-night, good-night!"

Such a number of rooks came over her head,
Crying, "Caw! caw!" on their way to bed;
She said, as she watched their curious flight,
"Little black things, good-night, good-night!"

The horses neighed, and the oxen lowed,
The sheep's "Bleat! bleat!" came over the road;
All seeming to say, with a quiet delight,
"Good little girl, good-night, good-night!"

She did not say to the sun, "Good-night!"
Though she saw him there like a ball of light;
For she knew he had God's time to keep
All over the world, and could never sleep.

The tall pink foxglove bowed his head,
The violet curtsied and went to bed;
And good little Lucy tied up her hair,
And said on her knees her favorite prayer.

And while on her pillow she softly lay,
She knew nothing more till again it was day,
And all things said to the beautiful sun,
"Good-morning! good-morning! our work is begun!"

—*Lord Houghton*

ULYSSES AND THE BAG OF WINDS

Long, long ago, there lived upon a little island a Greek king named Ulysses. One time Ulysses sailed far away across the sea to fight for his country. Ten long years he was away from his beautiful wife and his little son.

At last the Greeks captured the city they were fighting against, and the war ended. "Now I can go back to my island home," said Ulysses, joyfully, as he and his men set sail for home. "Once more I can see my wife and son!"

On the way, they stopped to rest at the home of a king named Aeolus, who lived on an island in the sea. It was a wonderful island; all around it was a high wall of bronze.

Aeolus was king of the winds. He could make the winds sleep so soundly that the sea would be as smooth as glass, or he could make them blow so hard that the waves would be as high as mountains.

When Ulysses was ready to start on his way again, Aeolus said, "I will help you to reach your home, Ulysses. I will put all the stormy winds in this great bag of ox-hide. Then they cannot harm you.

"I will tie the bag with this golden chain; but will leave out the gentle west wind, to bear you safely home. Guard the bag of winds carefully, and do not let anyone untie the chain."

Then the west wind blew softly and sent them in safety on their way. For nine days and nights Ulysses guarded the bag of winds, until at last he became very tired and sleepy.

Now the men with Ulysses did not know what was in the great bag. "See how he guards it!" they said. "Surely it has gold and silver in it, for it is tied with a golden chain. We helped Ulysses in the war; why should he have all the gold and silver?"

At last, on the tenth day, they came in sight of their dear island. "Look, look!" cried the men joyfully. "There are our green fields! Soon we shall see our homes."

Then the weary Ulysses, thinking that he need not guard the bag any longer, fell fast asleep.

"Now we can see what is in the bag!" said his men. " We can get some of the gold and the silver for ourselves."

So they crept up to the bag and untied the golden chain. Out flew all the stormy winds, roar-

ing and howling! In a moment, great waves arose
and drove the ship far from land.

The noise of the wind and the waves awoke Ulysses. Where was his little island home? Where were
the green fields he loved so well? They were far, far
away, for the ship was out on the stormy sea.

"Oh, what shall I do?" cried Ulysses. "I fear that
I shall never see my home again. But I must not
give up; I will try again and again. Some day I
may reach my home, and see my wife and son once
more."

After a long time, the stormy winds drove the
ship back to the island where Aeolus lived. How

glad Ulysses was when he saw the high wall of bronze! "Aeolus can help us," he said. "He will tie the winds again."

But Aeolus was angry with Ulysses and his men. "Go away!" he said. "I will not help you a second time, for it is your own fault that the stormy winds are out of the bag."

So once more Ulysses set out upon the sea, and it was many long years before he saw his island home again.

—*Greek Legend*

WHICH WIND IS BEST?

Whichever way the wind doth blow,
Some heart is glad to have it so;
And blow it east or blow it west,
The wind that blows, that wind is best.

—*Caroline A. Mason*

THE STAR AND THE LILY

Once upon a time all the people in the world were happy. No one was ever hungry; no one was ever sick. The beasts all lived together in peace; the birds all sang joyfully; the air was full of the sweetness of flowers; and every tree and bush gave fruit.

In this happy time the Indians lived a free life in the open air. At night they used to meet in the wide green fields and watch the stars.

One night the Indians saw a star that shone more brightly than all the others. It seemed very near to them, as it hung in the southern sky, close to the mountainside.

"It looks like a ball of fire," said the children. "See! It moves! It is a ball! Or is it a fiery bird flying to the mountain?"

"My father once told me of a moving star," said a wise old man. "It left its home in the sky to tell of war, and it always moved right across the heavens. A fiery cloud of arrows streamed far behind it. But no arrows follow this star. It cannot be the star of war."

That night a young warrior had a dream. He dreamed that he climbed the mountainside to find the strange star. And when he found it, the star changed to a beautiful maiden who came and stood by his side.

"I love this beautiful land," said the maiden. "I love its rivers and lakes and mountains. I love its birds and flowers. But more than all, I love its children. Young warrior, ask your wise old men where I may live so that I shall see the children always."

The next night, as the Indians sat in the wide green field watching the star, the young warrior told of his dream.

"Tell the star," said the wise old men, "that it will be welcome to live wherever it wishes."

So the star came to live upon the earth. At first it made its home in the white rose on the mountainside. But it was lonely there, for no child came near it.

"The children play in the wide green fields," said the star. "I must find a home where I shall be close to them."

Then it went down into the prairie and lived with one of the creatures of the air. "I will live in the air and yet upon earth," it said. "I will fly about with this happy little air-creature. Then I can see my sister-stars in the sky, and at the same time I can see the children at their play upon the earth."

But the little air-creature flew about only at dusk, so the star never saw the children.

"I am not happy," said the star. "I must find a home where the stars in the sky and the children upon the earth, all can be my playmates. But men shall know that the little air-creature once had a star for its friend."

And since that time, the firefly always carries a little star of fire.

Then the star floated away until at last it reached a beautiful lake. It looked down into the quiet water, and there it saw thousands of the stars of the sky.

"At last I know where to make my home," said the star. " I will live upon this lake. By day, I can see the children paddling in their canoes, or playing on the banks. By night, my sister-stars of the sky will come to stay beside me on the quiet water."

The next morning, two Indian children came paddling out in their canoe. Suddenly they saw a beautiful water lily, blooming upon the lake.

"A star! a star!" cried the children. "A star has come to live upon the water!"

"The star has found a home," said the wise old men. "We will call it the star-flower."

Every day the happy star-flower watched the children at their play. And at night, all about it in the still waters, were its sister-stars of the sky.

—*Old Indian Legend*

LITTLE PAPOOSE

Rock-a-by, hush-a-by, little papoose,
    The stars come into the sky,
The whip-poor-will's crying, the daylight is dying,
    The river runs murmuring by.

The pine trees are slumbering, little papoose,
    The squirrel has gone to his nest,
The robins are sleeping, the mother bird's keeping
    The little ones warm with her breast.

Then hush-a-by, rock-a-by, little papoose,
    You sail on the river of dreams;
Dear Manitou loves you and watches above you
    Till time when the morning light gleams.

—Charles Myall

PEBOAN AND SEEGWUN

It was very cold, and a strong wind was blowing The brooks and the lakes were covered with ice, and all the trees were bare. Not a sound was to be heard except the whistling of the wind.

All alone in a wigwam sat an old Indian. He was so old that his hair was as white as the snow outside. The fire in the wigwam was very low, and the old man sat near it, holding his hands out to the tiny blaze.

He was so weak that he could no longer leave the wigwam. Day after day he sat by the fire, thinking of the great deeds he had done when he was young.

Suddenly an Indian youth, tall and strong, stood at the opening of the wigwam. There was a glow upon his cheeks, and his hair was like sunshine.

"Come in!" said the old man. "It is cold outside. Stay here tonight with me."

So the young man came into the wigwam and sat down by the fire.

"Let us tell of the great deeds that we have done," said the old man. "When I blow my breath, the streams stand still, and the water is turned to ice."

"When I blow my breath," said the young man, "the ice melts, and the streams begin to flow."

"When I shake my white hair," said the old man, "snow fills the air, and the birds fly far away."

"When I shake my golden hair," said the youth, "the air is full of sunshine; the birds come back, and the trees burst into leaf."

"When I walk upon the earth," said the old man, "the ground becomes hard, and the flowers die."

"Wherever my foot touches the ground," said the young man, "it grows soft and warm again. Flowers spring up, and the grass becomes fresh and green."

So they talked all through the long night. When morning came, the cold wind was no longer blowing.

The sun was warm, and the bluebirds were singing joyfully.   Inside the wigwam the air grew
warmer and warmer.

After a time the young man arose. He looked
taller and stronger and more beautiful than ever.
But the old man lay by the fireside, sad and weak.
The fire was almost out.

"Youth, I know you now," said the old man. "You
are Seegwun, the Spring. I am Peboan, the Winter.
Once I could do great deeds, but now I am old and
weak. You are greater than I."

And all at once the old man was nowhere to be
seen; he had gone. But where his fire had been a
beautiful flower was growing.

It was the arbutus, the flower that seems to
belong both to winter and to spring. For it loves
the cold so much that it blooms while patches of
snow are still upon the ground. Its petals are
always rosy with the last gleams of Peboan's fire.

Yet it is always the first of the flowers to welcome Seegwun, the Spring.

—*Old Indian Legend*

A THANKSGIVING FABLE

It was a hungry pussy cat,
  Upon Thanksgiving morn,
And she watched a thankful little mouse
  That ate an ear of corn.

"If I ate that thankful little mouse
  How thankful he should be,
When he has made a meal himself,
  To make a meal for me!

"Then with his thanks for having fed,
  And his thanks for feeding me,
With all his thankfulness inside,
  How thankful I shall be!"

Thus mused the hungry pussy cat,
  Upon Thanksgiving Day;
But the little mouse had overheard
  And declined (with thanks) to stay.

—Oliver Herford

LITTLE PUMPKIN'S THANKSGIVING

Little Pumpkin's Wish

It was the night before Thanksgiving. The Great Big Pumpkin, the Middle-Sized Pumpkin, and the Little Wee Pumpkin were talking together in Peter Pumpkin-Eater's patch.

The Frost King had sent each of them, as a Thanksgiving gift, a pretty white coat that sparkled in the moonlight.

"Are all here?" asked the Great Big Pumpkin.

"All here," said the Middle-Sized Pumpkin, smiling.

"All here," said the Little Wee Pumpkin, sneezing, for the night air was chilly. "But I think it will be our last night together, for I heard Peter say today that tomorrow he would send us on our journeys. How delightful that will be!"

"To be sure," said the Great Big Pumpkin. "I hope we will make the best of pies for somebody's

Thanksgiving dinner.   Speaking of journeys, though, I do hope Peter will send me to the great city. They say the sights there are wonderful."

"So I have heard," said the Middle-Sized Pumpkin. "I should be glad to see the tall buildings there."

"And I, too," said the Little Wee Pumpkin. "I should like so much to see the Princess Cinderella, whom everybody loves. But I am not large enough or fine enough for her. Most of all, I should like to make some little child very happy on Thanksgiving Day. Then, too, I hope my seeds will be saved and planted next year. It is such a pleasant thing to grow!"

"Indeed it is!" said the Great Big Pumpkin.

"Indeed it is!" said the Middle-Sized Pumpkin.

"I wish Peter could plant all our seeds, for he takes such good care of us, and he likes so much to see us grow."

"Well, good-night and pleasant dreams," said the Great Big Pumpkin. "If we pumpkins do not soon go to sleep, the sunbeams will catch us napping, a pretty sight for a Thanksgiving morning!"

So the three pumpkins snuggled beneath their frosty coats and went to sleep.

THE WISH COMES TRUE

The next morning was Thanksgiving, and the Little Wee Pumpkin was the first to awake. She almost lost her breath with surprise when Peter opened the garden gate, and the Princess Cinderella herself tripped in behind him.

She was very beautiful. She had the same sunny hair and dainty feet and smiling face that you have read about. She was as good and as kind as ever.

In her hand she held a bunch of violets, almost the color of her pretty eyes. As she held them up to Peter, she smiled and said, "See! Peter, I have brought you these flowers from my beautiful gardens. They are my Thanksgiving gift to you.

"Now, Peter, you must help me to find the best pumpkin in all your garden, for a jack-o'-lantern. I know a little girl whom I can make very happy with a jack-o'-lantern. She has been sick a long, long time in the hospital, and I have promised her one for Thanksgiving Day."

"Yes, my lady," said Peter, bowing. And they went from vine to vine, hunting the best pumpkin. First the princess came to the Great Big Pumpkin;

but she would not take that—it was too large.
Then she came to the Middle-Sized Pumpkin, but
that was too large, also. And then she came to the
Little Wee Pumpkin, and that was just right!

Now the Little Wee Pumpkin was very much surprised when Cinderella stooped down and said
gaily, "You dear Little Wee Pumpkin! You will make
a most beautiful jack-o'-lantern! You are the very
one to make the little girl happy this Thanksgiving Day. Come, Peter, I have chosen this one," she
said, gently patting the Little Wee Pumpkin.

"Yes, my lady," said Peter. So he carefully tucked
the Little Wee Pumpkin into Cinderella's coach.
Away they whirled, off to the little sick girl.

While they were on their way to the hospital, the
princess made the Little Wee Pumpkin into a wonderful jack-o'-lantern. It had great round eyes as
big as silver dollars. As for its mouth, you could
never guess how it looked.

The Little Wee Pumpkin that Cinderella had made
into a jack-o'-lantern happened to think of the joy it
would bring to the little girl. Then the corners of its
mouth turned up in the most beautiful smile you ever
saw! It was as happy as it could be.

All this time the little sick girl lay in her bed, longing for the Thanksgiving jack-o'-lantern that the princess had promised her.

Suddenly the door opened, and in came Cinderella with the Little Wee Pumpkin. "Oh, my jack-o'-lantern!" cried the sick girl joyfully. "My beautiful jack-o'-lantern! Oh, look, Cinderella, see how it smiles at me!"

And the smile on the face of the Little Wee Pumpkin grew brighter and brighter. For it had wished to make some little child very happy on Thanksgiving Day, and its wish had come true.

—*Madge A. Bingham—Adapted*

A CHRISTMAS WISH

I'd like a stocking made for a giant,
    And a meeting-house full of toys;
Then I'd go out in a happy hunt
    For the poor little girls and boys;
Up the street and down the street,
    And across and over the town,
I'd search and find them every one,
    Before the sun went down.

One would want a new jack-knife
    Sharp enough to cut;
One would long for a doll with hair,
    And eyes that open and shut;
One would ask for a china set
    With dishes all to her mind;
One would wish a Noah's ark
    With beasts of every kind.

Some would like a doll's cook-stove
    And a little toy wash-tub;
Some would prefer a little drum,
    For a noisy rub-a-dub;

Some would wish for a story-book,
  And some for a set of blocks;
Some would be wild with happiness
  Over a new tool-box.

And some would rather have little shoes,
  And other things warm to wear;
For many children are very poor,
  And the winter is hard to bear;
I'd buy soft flannels for little frocks,
  And a thousand stockings or so,
And the jolliest little coats and cloaks
  To keep out the frost and snow.

I'd load a wagon with caramels
  And candy of every kind,
And buy all the almond and pecan nuts
  And taffy that I could find;
And barrels and barrels of oranges
  I'd scatter right in the way,
So the children would find them the
    very first thing
  When they wake on Christmas Day.

—Eugene Field

GRETCHEN'S CHRISTMAS

THE EMPTY SHOES

It was almost Christmas time, when one of the great ships that sail across the sea came into an American harbor. It brought a little girl named Gretchen, who had come with her father and mother to find a new home in our land.

Gretchen knew all about the story of Christmas. She had heard it over and over in her home across the sea.

Every year, a little before Christmas, she had placed her shoes in the garden so that Rupert could fill them. For in her country, children believe that Santa Claus has a helper, named Rupert. Every year, too, Gretchen had found a Christmas tree lighted for her on Christmas Day.

As she came across the ocean, she wondered what Christmas in the new country would be like. She wondered still more, when they reached a great city, and their boxes were carried up to a little room in a boardinghouse.

Gretchen did not like the boardinghouse; she could not feel at home there. But worst of all, her father became ill the day after they reached the big city.

It is not pleasant to be up so high in a boarding-house (even if you do seem nearer the stars) when someone you love is sick. Then, too, Gretchen began to think that Rupert had forgotten her. For when she set her little wooden shoes outside the door, they were never filled with goodies.

The tears would roll down Gretchen's fat, rosy cheeks, and fall into the empty shoes. She began to think that the people in America did not keep Christmas. How she wished she was in her old home again!

A kind woman in the boardinghouse felt sorry for the lonely little girl who could not speak English. So one day she asked Gretchen's mother if Gretchen might go with her to see the beautiful stores. She was a poor woman, who had no presents to give away; but she knew how to be kind. So she took the little girl by the hand and smiled at her very often as they hurried along the crowded street.

THE WISHED-FOR DOLL

It was the day before Christmas, and Gretchen was jostled and pushed by the crowds of people. At last they went into a store which made her blue eyes open wide, for it was a toy store—the most beautiful one she had ever seen.

In that store were toys that had come across the sea, as Gretchen had done. There were dolls from France, that were spending their first Christmas away from home. There were woolly sheep, and painted soldiers, and dainty furniture, and wonderful toys from many different lands.

Oh, it was splendid to be in the toy shop the day before Christmas! All the tin soldiers stood up so straight and tall. They looked as if they were just ready to march, whenever the big drums should call them.

The rocking-horses were waiting to gallop away. The tops were all ready to spin, and the balls rolled

about, because it was so hard for them to keep still.

The beautiful dolls were dressed in their best. One of them was a princess, who wore a white satin dress, and had a crown on her head. She sat on a throne in one of the windows, with all the other dolls around her.

It was in this very window that Gretchen saw a baby doll that made her forget all the others. It was a real baby doll, not nearly so fine as some of the others, but it had a look on its face as if it wanted to be loved. Gretchen's warm heart went out to it; for little mothers are the same all over the world. Such a dear baby doll! If Rupert ever came to this strange America, he would surely give it to her.

She thought about it all the way home, and all day long.

THE GOOD SAINT NICHOLAS

Although Gretchen's father was now better, her mother told her sadly that there could be no Christmas tree for them this year. The little girl tried to be brave. She wrapped herself up in a shawl, and, taking her shoes in her hand, crept down the stairs. Through the door she went and out upon the wooden porch.

There had been a light fall of snow that day, and yet it was a mild Christmas. Gretchen set her shoes evenly together, and then sat down near them; for she had made up her mind to watch them until Rupert came by.

All over the city the bells were ringing—calling "Merry Christmas" to each other and to the world. So sweetly did they sing to little Gretchen that they sang her to sleep that Christmas Eve.

In another part of the great city, that night, a little American girl named Margaret found her heart so filled with love and joy that she wanted to make everybody happy. All day long she had been doing loving deeds, and in the evening she started out with a basketful of toys to help Santa Claus.

Her father was with her, and they were so happy that they sang Christmas carols as they went along the street. They happened to pass in front of the wooden porch, just after Gretchen had fallen asleep by her empty shoes.

The moon had seen those empty shoes, and was filling them with moonbeams. The stars had seen them, and were peeping into them with pity. When Margaret and her father saw them, they stopped in surprise. They had been in lands across the sea, so they knew that the little owner was waiting for the good Saint Nicholas to come, or Rupert, his helper.

"What can we give her?" whispered Margaret's father, as he looked into her basketful of toys. But Margaret knew; for she took from the basket a baby doll—one that looked as if it wanted to be loved, and laid it tenderly beside the wooden shoes.

When Gretchen awoke, she did not see Margaret and her father, for they had gone. But, oh! what a wonderful thing she did see! There, beside the wooden shoes, lay the dearest Christmas gift that ever came to a homesick little girl in a strange country.

All the bells were ringing! Margaret and her father, as they went on their way, answered them with a merry Christmas carol:

> "Carol, brothers, carol!
> Carol merrily!
> Carol the glad tidings,
> Carol cheerily!"

—*Maud Lindsay—Adapted*

THE CHRISTMAS TREE

You come from a land where the snow lies deep
In forest glade, on mountain steep,
Where the days are short and the nights are long,
And never a skylark sings his song.
Have you seen the deer in his mountain home,
And watched the fall of the brown pine cone?

Do you miss your mates in the land of snow,
Where none but the evergreen branches grow?
Dear tree, we will dress you in robes so bright
That ne'er could be seen a prettier sight;
In glittering balls and tinkling bells,
And the star which the story of Christmas tells.

On every branch we will place a light
That shall send its gleam through the starry night;

And the little children will gather there,
And carol their songs in voices fair;
And we hope you will never homesick be,
You beautiful, beautiful Christmas tree.

—*Mary A. McHugh*

WHERE DO THE OLD YEARS GO?

Pray, where do the Old Years go, Mamma,
When their work is over and done?
Does somebody tuck them away to sleep,
Quite out of the sight of the sun?

Was there ever a year that made a mistake,
And stayed when its time was o'er,
Till it had to hurry its poor old feet,
When the New Year knocked at the door?

I wish you a Happy New Year, Mamma—
I am sure new things are nice—
And this one comes with a merry face,
And plenty of snow and ice.

But I only wish I had kept awake
Till the Old Year made its bow,
For what it said when the clock struck twelve
I shall never find out now.

—*Margaret E. Sangster*

AN EASTER SURPRISE

The Little Gardener

It was a sunny morning in the early springtime. The birds had not yet come back from the South, and the trees had no leaves. But the sun was warm and bright, and seemed to be trying to tell the world that winter was over.

Little Paul walked slowly up and down in front of his house, enjoying the pleasant sunshine. By and by he called out, "Oh, Mother! I wish I had something to play with!" So his mother brought him an old spoon from the kitchen, and a flowerpot full of sand from the cellar. She left him playing happily in the front yard while she went on with her work indoors.

Every year mother had a large bed of beautiful tulips that bloomed in the early spring. Of course, Paul did not know about the tulips, for he was only three years old; but he saw the big round place in the front yard, where there was no grass, and it looked nice and soft to dig in.

So he emptied his pot of sand into his little wagon, and filled it up again with soft dirt from the tulip bed. Then he emptied it into his wagon. Over and over again he did this, until his wagon was quite full.

"I shall have to take my load somewhere," he said to himself. "Where can I go with it?"

The long street was very quiet, and as nobody was in sight, the little boy walked slowly down to the corner. Just around the corner was a very small house where lived an old man and his wife.

The house had a wee front yard, and right in the middle of it was a round flower bed. Paul walked into the yard and, sitting down on the ground, began to dig with a sharp stick that he had found.

Underneath the dirt in Paul's wagon were some round brown things that had been in his mother's tulip bed. When Paul had made a little round hole in the flower bed, he put one of the queer brown things into it and covered it over. Then he made more round holes, and put into them all of the brown balls that were in his wagon. "I will put them in a straight row like soldiers," he said. After emptying the dirt from his wagon, he smoothed it over with his big spoon and started back home.

The Easter Tulips

Now it happened that the old man who lived in the little house was very, very ill. That afternoon the little old lady who lived there, too, sat looking out of the window.

"We'll have no flowers in our garden this year," she said to herself. For she knew that the old man would not be able to plant the seeds, as he had done for years and years. She felt very sad.

Following this sunny day, there were several rainy days, by and by a snowy one, and then many more that were warm and sunny. One happy day the old man was better, and the little old lady sat down for a moment's rest. She happened to look out of the window at her flower bed, and what should she see but something growing!

It must be weeds," she said, but she put her shawl over her head and ran out to see. How her eyes did shine when she found not weeds, but a row of tulips almost ready to bloom. "Oh, oh, oh!" she cried, "how did they ever get here? What a beautiful surprise they will be for Father!"

On Easter Day an armchair was pushed over to the window, for the old man was able to sit up for

an hour. The little old lady could hardly wait until everything was ready for her to pull back the curtain so that he could look out.

At last all was ready. "Why, Mother!" cried the old man. "Where did you get them?" For tulips were in full bloom, and oh, such beautiful ones! Red, yellow, pink, and white they were, swaying in the warm spring breeze.

"I do not know where they came from," she said, looking at the flowers with eyes full of happiness. "They are our Easter surprise."

"Somebody must love us, even if we are old and poor," said the old man.

"I never was so happy in my life," said the little old lady softly.

—*Louise M. Oglevee—Adapted*

OLD APPLESEED JOHN

The Kind Old Man's Plan

Once there was an old man, who lived in a queer little hut near a village. He did all kinds of jobs for the people who lived near him. His back was bent from hard work, but his heart was very kind.

Now this kind old man always wanted to make other people happy. One warm spring day he sat by the door of his queer little hut, eating an apple that he had bought for two pennies. As he sat there, he thought and thought and thought.

"What can I do to make others happy?" he said to himself. "It takes a great deal of money to do much good. But there surely must be some way for me to help others."

All at once a smile came over his face, and he clapped his hands like a boy. "Now I know what I can do," he said to himself. "It is so simple that I wonder I never thought of it before." When he had finished eating his apple, he put the core safely away and went to the village to find work.

Everywhere he worked, he asked the people to give him a part of his pay in apples. Taking these home, he ate them for his supper, and put the cores into a big bag in his hut. This he did every day.

The people in the village thought he was a very queer old man. "I think he is crazy," said a woman one day, as he passed by.

Some boys who were playing near heard her. "He is not crazy," said the boys; "and he is just as kind as he can be. We like to play around his little hut, for he tells us funny stories and sings us funny songs. We call him Appleseed John, because he saves all his apple-cores and puts them into a big bag. When we ask him what he wants them for, he just smiles and smiles, and says, 'When you have grown older, ask your children.'"

Apple-Seed John at Work

At last, one summer day, when the bag was quite full of apple-cores, Appleseed John shut the door of his little hut and walked away. In one hand he carried a long, pointed cane, and on his back a bag of apple-cores. His face was very, very happy. For miles and miles he walked, whistling as he went along. Every little while he would stop and make a hole in the ground with his cane. Then he would drop an apple-core into the hole and cover it over,

knowing that the sun and the rain would do the
rest. He sang merrily as he walked along, and this
is what he sang:

> "Old Appleseed John has work to do,
> And he must go on to carry it through."

All summer long he wandered far and wide, plant-
ing his apple-cores in the fields and along the roadsides. Everyone he met liked him, because he was
so kind and merry.

Sometimes, when he stopped at a farmhouse to
work for a few days, the farmer would say to him,
"Stay and work for me always. I will give you
a good bed and pay you well." But the old man
would shake his head and say:

> "Old Appleseed John has work to do,
> And he must go on to carry it through."

In this way the kind old man spent the rest of
his life. Years passed away, and the trees grew
and grew until they were big and strong. Every
autumn they were covered with wonderful apples.
Travelers, passing through the fields and along the
roadsides, rested in the shade of the trees, and ate
the fine, juicy fruit.

"These are surely the finest apples that ever grew," they would say. "How nice it is to see apple trees growing along the roadside. Who could have planted them here?" Then someone would tell them the happy story of old Appleseed John.

—*Lydia Maria Child—Adapted*

COLUMBUS AND HIS SON, DIEGO

A Place of Rest by the Roadside

One day, more than four hundred years ago, a man and a boy were walking along a dusty road in Spain. For a long time they had been traveling in the hot sun, and now they were tired and thirsty.

At last, as they came to a bend in the road, they saw a long, low building. "Diego," said the man "we will ask the good friars at that convent for a cool drink of water. They will let us rest there, and it may be that they can help me get ships for my great voyage. I can then prove that the world is round."

"I shall be glad to rest, Father, for I am very tired," said the boy. "But why do you think the friars can help you? You have asked many people for help, but no one has been willing to give you money or ships!"

It is true, Diego," said his father, "that the kings and the rich men have been unwilling to aid me. But I shall never give up hope. These good friars are wise and kind. They spend their lives in this convent, reading and studying all that has been written down in books.

"Surely they will be able to see that my plan will lead to great things. I have heard, too, that one of these friars, named Perez, is a friend of Isabella, the queen of Spain. He might ask her to let me have ships for my voyage."

So Columbus, for that was the name of Diego's father, knocked at the convent door. The friar who opened the door saw at a glance that the thoughtful looking man and his bright-faced boy were no common beggars. They were allowed to rest in the convent, and food and water were brought to them. Then the friars gathered around Columbus and asked him to tell them his story.

In those days, almost everyone except Columbus thought that the earth was flat. So when he tried to get ships for a long voyage to prove that the earth is round, men laughed at him and were unwilling to give him aid.

He told the eager friars who gathered around him how long he had tried to get help. Then, spreading out a rough map upon the table, Columbus pointed to India, far away to the east.

"If I can only get ships to sail in," he said, "I will prove that the world is round. For I will sail westward over the ocean. When I have sailed a long time, I shall come to India on the other side of the world. After that, the rich spices and the beautiful silks of India will be brought to Europe in ships. We shall no longer need to reach India by the slow caravans that take so long to travel by land."

All the friars looked at the map with interest. But Perez was even more eager than the others, for he had always been greatly interested in maps. "Columbus, you are right!" he suddenly cried. "I believe in your plan. I believe that you will find riches and lands across the sea for Spain. This very day I will send a messenger to Queen Isabella, asking her to give you ships for your voyage."

And so it came about that the queen of Spain gave Columbus the help for which he had waited so long. Early one August morning in the year 1492, he set sail with three ships from the coast of Spain.

DIEGO AS A PAGE AT THE PALACE

Little Diego wanted to go on the great voyage, but his father told him that he was too young. So the little boy was taken to the palace of the king of Spain, where he was to be a page until his father returned.

There were many unhappy hours in store for the lonely young boy, for almost everyone in Spain believed that Columbus would come to his death on his strange voyage. People called him "The Mad Sailor," because he said that the world is round and that he could reach India by sailing west.

Very often the other pages in the royal palace would draw around Diego and tease him. "Ho, Diego!" cried one of these boys about seven months after Columbus had sailed away. "What news today from The Mad Sailor?"

"When it is time for news from my father,"
answered Diego, drawing himself up proudly, "it
shall be great news, I promise you!"

"Time!" cried one of the others. "It is nearly
seven months since The Mad Sailor started out
from Palos! Isn't seven months enough time? Long
before this your father reached the edge of the
world and sailed right over it. Down, down, down,
he fell, he and his ships and his men!"

"The earth is round!" replied Diego. "There is
no edge to sail over. It is only foolish people who
think that the earth is flat. My father will sail on
and on until he reaches land on the other side of
the world!"

"Ho-ho-ho!" laughed all the other boys. "The
earth round! Ho-ho-ho!"

"Everyone knows that the earth is flat, and that
it rests upon the back of a great turtle!" said one of
the pages. "And there are terrible monsters in the
Sea of Darkness. They will swallow your father's
three ships at one mouthful."

"It is not so," replied Diego, with scorn. "All
around the world the sea is just the same blue
water that we see on our own shores. Far to the

west are wonderful islands. Farther still are the shores of India. My father will find them!"

Suddenly a messenger ran into the hall where the boys were talking. "Diego, the son of Columbus!" he called loudly. "Where is he? The queen sends for him! The great Columbus has found the land beyond the sea! A message has just come from him."

The pages fell back in surprise and shame as Diego proudly followed the messenger to the queen. In the whole world, there was no happier boy, for what his father had taught him was all true! The Mad Sailor had proved that the world is round!

The troubles of Diego were now over. Columbus had made his great voyage and had returned in safety. The king and queen of Spain gave him a royal welcome, and no honor was too great for The Mad Sailor, who had proved that the earth is round

Diego wept for joy when his father clasped him in his arms and told him the story of his adventures. And how his eyes opened when he saw the strange dark people, dressed in skins of wild beasts, that Columbus had brought with him from the lands beyond the sea!

We know now that it was not India that Columbus had found, but our own America. This great
land of ours, and the islands near it, lay right
across his path to the shore of India. But after
all, Columbus was right. For the earth is a globe,
and by sailing westward, around the world, we can
reach the lands in the far east.

—Sarah A. Haste

THE BOY, THE BEES, AND THE BRITISH

The Coming of the British

"I wish I could help General Washington, too, Mother! But here I must stay at home, while Father and brother Ben are fighting for our country."

Jack and his mother were sitting on the piazza of their Virginia home, one hot June day in the year 1781. There were hard times in Virginia that year, for British soldiers rode everywhere, seizing all the horses, and whatever they could find for food.

"You were left here to take care of me, Jack," said his mother. "The British have been here once already and have taken all our horses except Old Bay. They will surely come again. Would you want me to meet them alone?"

"No, indeed, Mother!" answered Jack, earnestly.

"I wouldn't leave you alone. But I wish I could fight for my country."

"Try to be contented, Jack," said his mother, gently. "Your brother Ben is in the army, and one boy is enough for me to spare just now. Wait until you are a little older."

"But I am nearly fifteen, Mother," pleaded Jack. "Father says that George Washington was only a boy when he went to fight the French and the Indians. And now he is general of all our army! Someday he will make our country free. How can anyone help his country by staying at home on a sleepy old plantation like this?"

Just then the clatter of horses' hoofs came to their ears from far down the road. Jack and his mother knew well enough what the sound meant.

"'The redcoats are coming!" cried the boy, jumping to his feet. "I'll get Old Bay out of the barn, Mother! The British shan't have our last horse if I can help it. I'll hide him back in the woods."

It did not take the young boy many minutes to hide Old Bay in a safe place. Then he ran back to the house as fast as his legs could carry him. "Now the old horse is safe, Mother," he said proudly.

"I am afraid, Jack," replied his mother, "that the British are after more than horses this time. Neighbor Green says their food is giving out. We'll not have much left to eat after this visit."

"Never mind, Mother!" said Jack. "If the redcoats take everything, I will see that you do not starve. I'm glad that I'm here, after all."

At that very moment, up the road with shouting and clatter of hoofs, came the British soldiers—four hundred of them. When they reached the plantation, they swarmed all over the place. They drove wagons into the yard and loaded them with corn from the barn and with food from the great cellar.

From the end of the piazza, Jack and his mother watched them. They saw the bellowing cattle driven up, and the squealing pigs taken from their pens. How the soldiers laughed and joked, as they chased squawking chickens about the yard!

"Hurry up, men!" called their leader. "And keep a sharp lookout. Don't let the rebels come upon us by surprise! Now get what horses you can find, and let us be off."

"It is hard, Jack," said his mother, as they heard these commands, "to see all our food taken in this way. I do not like to feed the British when our own soldiers are hungry."

"I am glad that I got Old Bay out of sight, anyway," said Jack, as he watched the soldiers.

JACK'S DARING PLAN

From his place on the piazza, Jack could see the barn, the long row of beehives near it, and the clump of bushes where Old Bay was hidden. Far beyond, stretched a long country road.

Jack's sharp eyes saw all these things at a glance. But they saw something else, too! Horsemen! Far down the road, horsemen were coming. And they were not redcoats this time; American soldiers were coming! Oh! if they could only get to the plantation in time to catch the British!

But the British lookouts had eyes as sharp as Jack's. Up went a shout, "The rebels! The rebels are coming!"

Suddenly a daring plan came into Jack's mind. "Run into the house, Mother," he whispered. "Quick! Quick!" Without stopping to explain his plan, he jumped from the piazza and ran toward the long row of beehives.

At that very moment, the horse-hunters rushed out of the barn, for they had heard the warning of the lookouts. Instantly, Jack picked up the nearest beehive and flung it into the midst of the hurrying soldiers. Then he ran like the wind to the place where Old Bay was hidden.

What a scene there was! The angry bees flew at men and animals, alike. Maddened by their stings, the horses plunged and kicked! The pigs and cattle and chickens joined in the uproar! Neighing, squawking, bellowing, squealing, and shouting filled the air!

The British soldiers ran wildly about, falling over each other in their efforts to beat off the stinging bees. "Run for it, men! Run for it!" shouted their leader. Then, helter-skelter they ran down the road, with the angry bees flying about their heads.

But they were too late. Their fight with the bees had delayed them, and the pain from the stings had confused them. In the meantime, Jack had jumped upon Old Bay's back and ridden away to tell the American soldiers where the British were. And at that very moment, flying along the road close behind them, came American troops—led by a boy on an old bay horse!

So it was that the brave young American boy found a way to help his country, even though he could not join Washington's army. For the four hundred British soldiers were captured, and it was Jack with his angry bees who brought it about.

—Lutie Andrews McCorkle—Adapted

WHY JIMMIE MISSED THE PARADE
ON WASHINGTON'S BIRTHDAY

It was the twenty-second of February, and the line was already forming for the parade in honor of George Washington. Bobbie and Jack and Jimmie were three happy boy scouts, and this was their first parade.

Last year they had stood on the curb and watched the other boy scouts march proudly past. But this year they were old enough to be scouts themselves, and good ones they were. They knew the scout laws and kept them, too.

They were standing in their places in the street, waiting anxiously for the parade to start. A company of soldiers, who had been fighting in France during World War One, stood in front of them. They were real heroes to the boy scouts, who felt proud to march behind them and the faded flag which they carried.

How happy and excited the boys were! The air was clear, the flags were flying, crowds of people were walking up and down the street, horses were prancing, and everything was gay.

"Oh, look! There goes the governor in that big automobile all covered with flags!" said Bobbie. "He is going to make a speech about George Washington after the parade is over, and my father is going to hear him. I'd like to be governor some day."

"I'd rather be president," said Jack. "Wouldn't you, Jimmie? "

But Jimmie did not answer. Jimmie was a very thoughtful little boy. He was thinking of the poem about George Washington that he had learned in school the week before, and he was saying it quietly to himself.

"It's splendid to live so grandly
  That long after you are gone
The things you did are remembered
  And recounted under the sun.
To live so bravely and purely
  That a nation stops on its way
And once a year with banner and drum
  Keeps its thoughts of your natal day."

"My!" thought Jimmie. "It is splendid to have everyone in the whole country celebrating your birthday with banners and drums and flags and processions!"

Just then a soldier blew a loud blast on a bugle, the band began to play, and the soldiers in front of the boy scouts began to move. "Forward, march!" said the Scout Master, and every boy except Jimmie obeyed.

Instead of marching forward, Jimmie suddenly darted across the street where a policeman's horse, frightened by the band, was prancing and rearing on his hind legs. Jimmie's sharp eyes had seen a poor little dog struck by the hard hoofs of the frightened horse. There the little animal lay in the street with one leg broken, stunned, and unable to move.

Jimmie caught up the little dog just in time to save him from being crushed by an automobile. But what could he do with him? He held him tenderly in his arms, while he wondered and wondered. The boy scouts were already half a block away, and no one on the sidewalk offered to take the poor little dog.

There was nothing for Jimmie to do but to carry the dog to his own home, which was six blocks away.   Of course he knew he would miss the parade, and oh, how bad he did feel about that!

He ran all the way home, made the little dog a soft bed in a box, and then started after the parade. But he was too late. He had lost so much time that when at last he caught up with the boy scouts, they had reached the end of the line of march. Oh, how disappointed he was!

That night there was a scout meeting and, of course, Jimmie went. He was a little late, for he had stopped to help his father set the little dog's broken leg. When he entered the room the boys all shouted, "Hurrah for Jimmie Preston. He's a good scout, all right!"

"Indeed he is," said the scout master. "'A boy scout is kind.' And today Jimmie Preston was both kind and brave."

"Just like George Washington when he was a boy," said Bobbie.

"Hurrah for George Washington, the best scout of all," said the boys.

—Edna V. Riddleberger

A LITTLE LAD OF LONG AGO

Little Abe hurried home one cold winter evening, as fast as his feet could carry him. Perhaps if he had worn stockings and shoes like yours, he could have run faster. But instead, he wore deerskin leggings and clumsy moccasins of bearskin that his mother had made for him.

Such a funny-looking boy he was, hurrying along across the rough fields! His suit was made of warm homespun cloth. His cap was made of coonskin, and the tail of the coon hung down behind.

But if you could have looked into the honest, twinkling blue eyes of this little lad of long ago, you would have liked him at once.

In one hand little Abe held something very precious. It was only a book, but the boy thought more of that book than he would have thought of gold or jewels.

You cannot know just what that book meant to little Abe, unless you are very fond of reading. Think how it would be to see no books except two or three old ones that you had read over and over, until you knew them by heart! So, when a neighbor had said that little Abe might take a book home with him, and keep it until he had read it all through, do you wonder that his eyes shone like stars?

Little Abe's home was not much like your home. It was not built of stone or brick, but of rough logs. When he lay in his small bed, close to the roof, he could look through the chinks between the logs and see the twinkling stars shining down upon him.

Sometimes the great yellow moon smiled at him as she sailed through the dark night sky. And sometimes, too, saucy raindrops pattered down upon the face of the sleeping boy.

Every night, after little Abe had crept up the steps to the loft, he put his precious borrowed book in a small crack between the logs. In the morning, when the first gray light came in, he awoke and read until his father called him.

Little Abe worked hard all day long. He never had a moment in the daytime to peep between the covers of his beloved book. So, night after night he read, until the book was nearly finished.

One night he slipped the book away as usual, and fell asleep to dream of the wonderful story. He awoke very early, but no golden sunbeams peeped at him through the chinks. The loft was dark and cold.

Little Abe reached out his hand for the book— and what do you think? He put it into a pile of something white and cold; for his bed was covered with a blanket of soft white snow!

He sat up shivering, and reached again for the book. When he pulled it out and saw how it looked, the poor little fellow almost cried. For that precious book was wet from cover to cover, and its crisp leaves were soaked with snow.

Poor little Abe! There was a big lump in his throat as he looked at the spoiled book, for what would its owner say? As soon as he was dressed, the young boy hastened to the kind neighbor. Looking straight into the man's face, he told his sad story.

"Well, my boy," said the man, "so my book is spoiled. Will you work to pay for it?"

"I will do anything for you," said the boy eagerly.

"Well, then, I will ask you to pull fodder-corn for three days," said the man.

Little Abe looked up into his kind neighbor's face. "Then, sir," he asked, anxiously, "will the book be mine?"

"Why, yes, of course," said the man, good-naturedly. "You will have earned it."

So little Abe worked for three days. He was cold, and his back often ached as he pulled the corn. But he was too happy to care about such things as these, for was not that precious book to be his very own?

What do you suppose the book was, for which little Abe worked so long and so faithfully? Was it a book of wonderful fairy tales? No; it was the story of George Washington's life.

Long afterwards, when little Abe had become the president of the United States, he used to tell the story of his first book. "That book—the life of George Washington—helped me to become president," said Abraham Lincoln.

—Alice E. Allen

JACQUES, A RED CROSS DOG

MY LIFE ON THE FARM

My name is Jacques, and I am just a plain shepherd dog. But I have done my bit for my country, and since many folks think dogs are not good for much, I'd like to tell you of the things that some of us did in World War One.

I lived with my kind master and his family in a little cottage in France about a mile from a big town. Besides my master and mistress, there were François, who was twelve years old; Nannette, who was eight; and little Jeanne, who was not quite two.

I was just an awkward puppy five months old, and I was always getting under somebody's feet and barking at the wrong time. I wouldn't like to tell you how many times I woke baby Jeanne from her nap. But I was learning a little every day, and master said I was very clever for my age.

We had only a little piece of land, with a horse, a cow, some rabbits, a few chickens, and a small garden. Still, we were a very happy family.

Then, suddenly, World War One came, and one sunny September day my good master went away to become a soldier, to fight for his little home and his country.

We all walked with him to the turn of the road, where he kissed my mistress and the children goodbye. Patting me on the head, he said, "Good Jacques, take care of my family until I come back." I knew right then that my puppy days were over, and that there was work for me to do.

We went back to the little farm, and all through the sunny days of autumn we worked very hard. François took old Hugo, the horse, and went off each day to gather wood for the winter. My mistress dug the vegetables from the little garden and stored them away in the cellar. Nannette took care of baby Jeanne. As for me, I tended Cosette, the cow, to keep her from straying too far from home while feeding on the grass along the roadside.

Sometimes our rabbits would get away, too, and I would have to help hunt for them, or we would have no rabbit stew in the cold winter months.

Every evening after work, François and I would walk to the big town a mile away, to hear the latest news of the war, and to see if there was a letter from my good master. If there was one, François would let me carry it home in my mouth, and it always made my mistress so happy that I longed for a letter every day.

As the winter went by, I felt myself growing stronger and stronger. Every day I learned something new. François always talked to me a great deal when we were working together, and so helped me to learn quickly the things that a dog ought to know.

My Training at the Dog War-School

Toward the end of winter it happened that my mistress had not had a letter for several weeks, so she was quite sad. Then, one day, while the family was at dinner, an airplane flew over our heads.

Looking up into the sky, I saw a white paper fluttering slowly downward. I watched to see where

it fell and dashed after it with a bark of joy, for I thought that it was a letter from my master. Looking off in the distance, I saw other papers fluttering down from the airplane, which I thought were more letters from other soldiers.

With the paper in my mouth, I rushed into the house to my mistress and proudly laid it at her feet, wagging my tail very hard in great joy. She took the paper in her hand, and this is what she read "Dogs are needed for the army. If you have a good dog, send him to a dog war-school, where he will be trained to serve his country."

My mistress looked at François, and François looked at her. Then, throwing his arms around my neck and bursting into tears, François said, "Good old Jacques, that means you." And it did.

The next day I sorrowfully followed François to town, where I was enrolled as a dog of war to work for France. The following day I was sent to a dog camp, where I found many dogs of different kinds being trained for work.

There were quick little terriers, who were being trained as rat hunters for the trenches. There were strong Airedales, who were being taught to stand guard, like real sentinels. There were swift-footed collies, who were learning how to carry messages. And the shepherd dogs, like myself, were being taught to do Red Cross work—to hunt for the wounded and dying on the battlefield, and to carry them food and drink and medicines in the little saddles which were strapped on our backs.

At first, the constant boom of guns around our camp made us very nervous, but we soon learned not to mind the noise. Of course, we didn't like the gas masks at all, as no dog likes to have his mouth covered.

But about the hardest thing we had to learn was to keep from barking. You see, a barking dog is dangerous in war, for he might make known the position of his own soldiers by even a very little bark. Barking is the joy of life for a dog, and to learn how to work silently was very, very hard.

The dogs that couldn't learn to do this were sent back to their homes. I could have gone back to our little cottage if I had barked as I worked, but I knew François would be ashamed of me. And, more than that, I should be ashamed of myself.

When our work became so easy that it was just like play, our training was over, and we were sent to the front to take our part in the great war.

How I Saved My Master

One cold, rainy evening, I was put into an ambulance with six other dogs and hurried to a part of the front where there had been a great battle. Our big ambulance went at great speed over the deep ruts in the road. Several times, I thought we should surely overturn.

We dogs were hurled from side to side and thrown against each other. One great plunge of the ambu-

lance threw three other dogs against me at once,
and I felt a sharp pain in my leg. But just then we
reached the battlefield, and I had no time to stop,
not even to give one little lick. For the great game
had begun for us, and we were eager to be in it.

Dashing over the field, where a few bullets were
still flying, we went searching for wounded soldiers.
I was the first to reach a big ditch. I heard a faint
cry and, looking down, I saw a man lying on his back
with a pile of earth over his legs. Sliding down, I soon
reached his side, and what was my surprise to look
into the face of my own good master!

I dared not bark, so I licked his face and his hands, and beat the air with my tail. Soon he opened his eyes and saw me. And, oh, joy! he knew me at once; for a good master always knows his own dog, just as a good dog always knows his own master.

"Good old Jacques," he said, "how did you ever get here?" And I thought my heart would burst with happiness.

I stood close by his side, so that he could help himself from my saddle pockets. "Come on the other side, old chap," he said. "This arm feels queer." So I went around to the other side, while he drank something from a little bottle that he found in one of my pockets.

Then, finding paper and a pencil, he wrote something on it. "A letter to my mistress," thought I. "I'll quickly take it to her." There was water in the ditch, and I was very thirsty from the pain in my leg, but I dared not stop to drink.

Taking the little letter in my mouth, I climbed out of the ditch, hurried across the field, which was quiet now, and almost dark, and found my way back to the ambulance. I dropped my letter at the feet of one of the stretcher-bearers, and in a short time I led the men back over the field to my dear master's side.

To make a long story short, we both went to the hospital, my master with a badly wounded arm, and I with a broken leg. It's funny how a dog's leg can be broken, and he not know it.

In a few weeks, however, my leg was well and strong again, and I went back to the front, where I helped save many other poor wounded soldiers. But my master was sent home.

The war is over now, and we are back at the little farm and are just as happy as we can be. To be sure, I am a little stiff and lame from cold and dampness, and my master has only one arm. But François is quite big enough now to take care of the little farm, and I can still tend Cosette.

François is proud of me because I was decorated several times. But I am proud only because I was able to save my master's life. That is worth more to me than many decorations.

—*Edna V. Riddleberger*

JOSEPH, THE RULER

Joseph and His Brothers

Little Joseph lived many years ago in the land of Canaan. All around his home were grass-covered hills, which made good pasture land for the sheep. Joseph's father was a rich man, who had large herds of cattle and flocks of sheep. His sons led these flocks to pasture every day and watched over them.

As Joseph grew older, his father sometimes allowed him to go out into the pastures with his ten big brothers. At first the brothers were very happy together, but after a time, some of the older boys began to think that their father loved Joseph more than he loved them.

One day Joseph went out into the fields, dressed in a beautiful new coat of many colors. His brothers looked at him in surprise, for none of them had such a coat as this. They wore sheepskin coats, and their arms were bare.

"See the new coat that father gave me!" said Joseph. "Is it not beautiful?"

"Yes, indeed!" said his brother Reuben, pleased because the young boy was happy. But the others were angry with their father for giving Joseph such a beautiful coat.

"Why should father give you such a coat as that?" asked one.

"We are older than you, and he has never given us coats of many colors," said another.

"Go home!" said a third brother. "We do not want you near us!"

"No, he will not go home!" said Reuben, putting his arm around Joseph. "He shall stay with me."

The other brothers were afraid to say more to Reuben, for he was the oldest of them all. So they walked away, looking back angrily at Joseph.

One night, soon after this, Joseph had a strange dream, and the next day he said to his brothers, "I dreamed last night that we were all in the fields, binding the sheaves of grain. Suddenly my sheaf stood up, and all your sheaves stood around it and bowed down to it. Was not that a strange dream?"

"I think it was a very strange dream!" said one brother, angrily. "I suppose you think that we shall bow down to you some day!"

"I never thought of your bowing down to me," said Joseph. "Do not be angry!"

But his brothers were angry, and they went out to the pastures, leaving him alone.

Joseph Is Sold as a Slave

One day the ten older brothers saw Joseph coming across the fields to them.

"Here comes Joseph, the dreamer," said one.

"He thinks he is better than we, because he wears fine clothes," said another. "I hate him!"

Then they planned how they might get rid of their younger brother. They knew that they could not harm Joseph while Reuben was with them, so they waited until he had gone away. Then they sold Joseph as a slave to some merchants who were passing by on their way to Egypt.

Upon their return home, they told their father that Joseph had been carried off by a wild beast.

When the merchants reached Egypt, they sold Joseph to one of the king's officers. This man soon found out that Joseph was faithful, and that he knew how to take care of sheep and cattle. Little by little he gave Joseph charge over all his flocks and his servants.

So faithful was the young slave that after a few years people began to hear of him—the wise, kind, honest Joseph, who was so different from all the people about him.

Now it happened that one night the king of Egypt had a strange dream. The next day he asked all his wise men what the dream meant. When no one could tell him, the king was very much troubled.

At last one of his servants said, "O King, I believe that Joseph, the wise slave, can tell you the meaning of your dream."

"Bring Joseph to me," said the king.

So Joseph was brought to the palace, and the great king of Egypt told him his dream.

"O King," said Joseph, "the meaning of your dream is this. For seven years, plentiful harvests will be gathered. Then will come seven years in which nothing will grow. God has told you this in a dream so that you may get ready for the seven years of famine. Then your people will not starve."

"But what can I do, Joseph?" asked the king.

"Choose a man who is wise and honest, O King," said Joseph. "Give him charge over all the land, and let him store up grain during the seven years of plenty. Then there will be storehouses full of corn in the years when no corn will grow."

Joseph Becomes a Ruler

"Joseph, you have shown that you are wiser than all my wise men," said the king. "You shall be ruler, for me, over all the land of Egypt. Tell the people what they must do to prepare for the seven years of famine. Your orders shall be obeyed, and all Egypt will love you and bless you."

The king then placed his own ring on Joseph's finger and threw a beautiful gold chain around his neck. He gave him clothes of fine linen and a chariot, just like his own. Whenever Joseph went out, servants ran before him, calling out to all the people, "Bow down before the great ruler of Egypt!"

When the seven years of plenty had passed, there came a time during which no crops would grow. There was no food in any land except Egypt, but in that country the storehouses were full of grain.

People came from other countries to Egypt to buy corn, and among them were Joseph's ten older brothers. Their father had heard that corn could be bought in Egypt, and so he sent them there to buy.

But he kept Benjamin, his youngest son, at home. "Joseph is dead," he said, "and I still mourn for him. Now if any harm should come to Benjamin, it would kill me."

His sons tried to comfort him, for they knew they had brought a great sorrow upon their father when they sold Joseph as a slave. They had never been able to forget their wicked deed, and they often thought how good they would be to their brother if he could come back to them.

Very sadly Joseph's brothers set out for Egypt, wondering if they should ever feel happy again. On their way to the great storehouses they heard a cry, "Bow down! Bow down! Here comes the great ruler of Egypt!"

They saw that all the people bowed with their faces to the ground, when they heard these words. The brothers, also, bowed down, just as a chariot drove swiftly past.

Then they stood up and followed the crowd of people who were going to buy corn. When their turn came to speak to the ruler, the brothers again bowed down to the ground.

They did not know that this great lord was the gentle little brother to whom they had said they would never bow down. But Joseph knew his brothers as soon as he saw them. He did not tell them who he was, for he said to himself, "I will find out first whether they still hate me."

When he had asked his brothers about their home and their family, he sold them some corn to take to their father. But he told them that he would not sell them any more, unless they brought their youngest brother to Egypt.

The brothers returned to their home with the corn, but it was not long before they needed more food. Then they told their father that they could buy no corn unless Benjamin went with them.

At first the poor old man would not allow Benjamin to go to Egypt, but at last when their food was nearly used up, he said that the young boy might go. "Be sure to bring him back safe," he said, "or I shall die. I am an old man, and Benjamin is my youngest and dearest son."

Joseph Forgives His Brothers

So once more the brothers set out for Egypt, and again stood before Joseph.

"Is your father well?" asked Joseph.

"Our father is in good health," they answered, bowing down to the ground.

"Is this your youngest brother? " asked Joseph.

"This is Benjamin," they answered, bowing.

"God bless you, my boy," said Joseph, putting his hand on his young brother's head. He could hardly keep himself from throwing his arms around Benjamin. But first he wanted to find out how his brothers felt toward him.

So Joseph sold them as much corn as they could carry. But the next morning, when they were ready to start home, he told them that he would keep their youngest brother as a slave.

Then one of the brothers fell on his knees before Joseph and said, "Oh, my brave Prince, keep me as a slave instead of Benjamin. We have been very wicked, and have caused our father great sorrow. Many years ago we hated our young brother, Joseph, so much that we sold him as a slave. Our father has mourned for him ever since, and from that day on, we have never been happy. Now, if harm should come to Benjamin, our father would die! We cannot go home without the boy!"

As he spoke, the poor man began to weep, and all the other brothers wept with him.

"Oh, my dear brothers!" cried Joseph, while the tears ran down his cheeks, too. "I am Joseph. Now I know that you love Benjamin, and I believe that you will love me."

"Are you Joseph?" asked one of the brothers. "Can you forgive us for our wickedness?"

"I forgave you long ago," said Joseph. "Do not weep any more, for God has blessed me in this land. If my father were only here, I should be perfectly happy!"

Before very long, Joseph had his wish, for his father came to Egypt and lived there, with his twelve sons around him. Then, Joseph was not only the greatest man in all Egypt, but also the happiest.

—*Clara E. Lynch*

DAVID, THE SINGER

David's Life as a Shepherd

"Mother, I wish I were old enough to go to war with my brothers! I do not want to take care of the sheep every day!" said a little boy in Bethlehem, many years ago.

"Is that what you have been thinking about, David?" asked his mother." I wondered why you had stopped singing."

"Yes. Our king is so good and so brave that I want to do something for him, to show him my love."

"I hope you will have a chance some time, David, but you must wait until you are older. Now get your harp and sing for me the beautiful song I heard you singing as you came home this evening."

"Did you like it, Mother? I made that little song out in the fields today. I was trying to thank God for taking care of me and my sheep."

Months passed, and David said no more about being a soldier, but went on faithfully with his work as a shepherd. Sometimes he went so far to find green pastures that he could not get home before dark. Then he would spend the night in the fields with his flock.

There was no sleep for David on these nights, for often he could hear the lions roaring. Hour after hour he would sit, watching to see that no harm came to his sheep.

One evening as David sat guarding his sheep, he heard a noise in the bushes not far away. Springing to his feet, he grasped his staff firmly and stood ready to fight for his flock. Suddenly, a great lion sprang out of the bushes and seized a lamb. Instantly, David rushed forward and struck the beast a heavy blow with his staff.

Roaring angrily, the lion dropped the lamb and leaped upon David. But the brave boy seized the lion's jaw with one strong hand, while with the other he struck such a blow that the great beast fell dead.

That night David played upon his harp and sang these words, " I will give thanks unto Thee, O Lord, and sing praises unto Thy name!"

Some months passed, and then one day David saw a number of men riding swiftly toward him. He knew at once that this was a band of robbers, who would try to kill him and carry off his sheep.

"I am only one, and they are many," he said to himself. "But I will not be afraid, for I know that God will help me."

So the brave young shepherd seized his sling and placed himself in front of his sheep. Then as the robbers came near, he shot one stone after another at them. With each shot, a rider fell from his horse.

Most of the robbers, thinking that there were a great number of men fighting against them, turned and fled. But some of them saw that David was alone. With a shout, they jumped from their horses and rushed toward the boy.

Then David raised his staff and struck such great blows that the robbers cried to one another, "The boy has the strength of a giant!" In great haste they ran to the spot where they had left their horses, and rode away.

DAVID HELPS KING SAUL

One evening not long after this, David's father told him that a strange illness had come upon King Saul, their ruler. At times he was so wild and fierce that no one dared to go near him.

All the next day, as David watched his sheep, he thought of his dear king. "If I were only near him, perhaps I could help him," thought the boy. "I would not be afraid."

While David was thinking about the king, some of the soldiers were talking together about his illness. "What can we do?" asked one of them. "King Saul will neither eat nor sleep."

"Perhaps music would quiet him," said the captain. "But who would dare sing or play before him? The king may throw his great spear at anyone who goes near him."

"Young David would not be afraid," said one of the soldiers. "He is not afraid of anything, and he has the sweetest voice you ever heard."

"Bring the boy to me," said the captain.

The next day a soldier took David to the captain. The great soldier looked at the brave young boy

and smiled. "David," he said, "it may be that I am doing wrong to send you before King Saul. He is so fierce in his illness that he may kill you."

"I am not afraid," answered David. "I shall be glad to try to help our poor king."

The king was sitting with bowed head when David entered the room and said gently, "I am David, dear King Saul. I have come to sing and to play for you."

The king did not lift his head or speak. He did not seem to know that anyone was near.

Then David drew his fingers gently over his harp, and sang in a low, sweet voice. Little by little, the frown left the king's face, and he lifted his head and looked at David.

Then David sang on and on. He sang of green pastures, and of the little brooks that ran through the fields. "O my King, do not be troubled! God will watch over you, as I watch over my sheep."

David ended his song, and for a while the room was very still. At last the king said, in a gentle voice, "Come here, my boy." When David went forward, Saul laid his hands upon the boy's shoulders. "You have helped me more than you know," said the king. "Will you stay with me always?"

"I must go back to my father and mother," answered David, "but I will come to you, dear King, whenever you wish."

That night, when David reached home, he cried joyfully to his father and mother, "At last I have been able to help my king!"

David and the Giant

Months passed, and David was still a quiet, faithful shepherd boy, spending his days in the fields with his sheep. One day his father said to him, "David, my son, take this corn and bread and cheese to your brothers and their captain." Very gladly the young boy started on his journey.

Now the army of King Saul was on a hill; the army of the enemy was on another hill, and there was a valley between them. As David came near, he heard a great shouting. Quickly he ran forward until he found his three older brothers, for he thought that the battle was beginning. But when he came to them, he was surprised to find that the battle had not begun. "What is the matter?" he asked. "Why does not the battle begin?"

"Look down there!" said one of the brothers.

David looked down and saw a strange sight. Between the two armies a great giant walked back and forth in the valley. His breast was covered with brass armor, and before him walked a man carrying his great shield.

As the young boy looked down, he heard the giant calling to Saul's army. "Choose a man to come down here and fight me!" he shouted. "You are all cowards and dare not fight me!"

"How dare he talk like that to the army of Israel?" cried David. "Surely there are brave men here who will fight him!"

"That is easy to say!" said a soldier who was standing near. "But who dares fight such a giant?"

"I do not fear him!" answered the brave young boy. "I will fight him!"

Some of the soldiers laughed at this, but one of them ran to King Saul, crying, "O King, at last we have found someone who is not afraid of the giant!"

"Bring him to me," said the king.

"O King," said David, when he stood before Saul, "I will fight this wicked giant."

"You cannot fight him," said Saul. "You are only a boy, and this great giant has fought many battles."

"I have fought a lion," answered David, "and God saved me from him. God will save me now from this enemy."

Then King Saul put his own armor upon David, and a helmet upon his head. "Go, then, my boy, and may God bless you!" he said, as he gave him his sword, also.

But when David tried to walk, he found that the armor was too heavy and that the sword was too long, for Saul was a very tall man. So David put off the armor. "I am a shepherd boy," he said. "I have my staff and my sling, and they are enough for me."

Then David picked up five smooth stones out of the brook and put them into his wallet. With his sling in his hand, he went down to meet the great giant.

"Who is this boy who comes to fight me with a stick?" roared the giant, when he saw the brave boy coming toward him. "I shall soon make an end of him!"

"You have sword and spear and shield," answered David. "But God will help me to win this battle and to save the people of Israel."

As he said these words, he ran forward and shot one of the stones from his sling. So sure was the young boy's aim, and so strong was his arm, that the stone struck the giant upon the forehead, and he fell dead.

Then a great shout went up from the army of Israel, and they rushed down into the valley and up the other hill. But faster still the enemy ran before them, for they dared not stand and fight when their greatest soldier was dead.

Never before had such a victory been won. "David is the greatest soldier in all the world!" cried the people joyfully.

In later years, David became king of Israel. Although he was a great warrior, he is remembered today, not for the battles he won, but for the songs he wrote.

For hundreds of years, men and women all over the world have read these songs and sung them. In times of sorrow, they bring cheer; in times of gladness, they help people to express their joy. So through all the years, people have found delight in these songs, which we call the "Psalms of David."

—*Clara E. Lynch*

THE BOY AND THE SHEEP

"Lazy sheep, pray tell me why
In the pleasant field you lie,
Eating grass and daisies white,
From the morning till the night.
Everything can something do,
But what kind of use are you?"

"Nay, my little master, nay;
Do not serve me so, I pray!
Don't you see the wool that grows
On my back, to make you clothes?
Cold, oh, very cold you'd be,
If you had no wool from me.

"True, it seems a pleasant thing,
To nip the daisies in the spring;
But many chilly nights I pass
On the cold and dewy grass,
Or pick a scanty dinner where
All the ground is brown and bare.

"Then the farmer comes at last,
When the merry spring is past,
And cuts my woolly fleece away,
For your coat in wintry day.
Little master, this is why
In the pleasant field I lie."

—*Jane Taylor*

SAINT GEORGE AND THE DRAGON

The Boy and the Plowman

"Oh, Father," cried a little boy, one day long ago, running up to the door of a cottage. "A splendid black horse just galloped by, and the man who rode him was shining so brightly that I could hardly look at him!"

"You saw one of the knights riding to the palace, George," said his father. "It was his armor that shone so brightly."

"What do knights do, Father?" asked the little boy.

"Good knights help people who are in trouble," the father answered, smiling at the eager child. "They ride all over the country, fighting wicked giants and punishing robbers."

"Oh, Father, do get a horse and be a knight! You are always helping poor people."

"I am only a poor plowman, George. I can never be a knight," said the father quietly.

"Never mind, Father," said George. "When I am a man, I will be a knight, and you may ride my horse."

"My poor little boy, how can you ever be a knight when your father is only a plowman?"

"I don't want to be a knight, Father, if the thought of it makes you sad. I want to stay with you always."

George and his father were very poor, but they were always happy together. Every evening the plowman would tell the little boy wonderful stories of fairies and giants. Once he told him of a baby who had been stolen from home and left in a field, where he was found by a poor plowman.

"The plowman lived alone," said his father, "and this was such a dear little baby that he soon learned to love him. He named the baby George, and when he went out to the fields he carried George with him. Before long the baby was a little boy, running after the plow, and calling the plowman 'Father.' "

"Why, Father," cried George, before his father could finish the story, "that is just like you and me!"

"Yes, George, because you were the dear little baby, and I am the plowman who found you. But I hope that some day you will find your own parents, for I know that they must be great people."

"I don't want to find them," said the little boy. "I want to stay with you, always!"

George Becomes a Knight

"Father," said George, one day, several years later, "I am tall and strong now. I want to go out and help someone who is in trouble. I know I can do good, even though I am not a knight."

"You are right, George, and I shall not keep you back. There is much evil in the world, and strong, brave men are needed to fight for those who cannot fight for themselves."

"Do you think the queen would send me to help someone, just as she sends her knights?"

"Go to the palace and ask her, my boy. This is the week of the great feast, and she will not refuse anything good that is asked at this time."

Early the next morning, George set out for the palace. When he entered the great hall, he walked straight up to the throne on which the queen sat and knelt before her.

"I wish to do a brave deed, gentle lady," he said. "I pray you give me the first chance that comes."

"You look very young," said the queen, "but I cannot refuse anything good that is asked during this feast. Wait here; your chance may come soon."

George had not been waiting long, when a beautiful princess named Una entered the hall. "O gentle Queen," she cried, "send one of your bravest knights with me to fight a dragon that has shut up my father and mother in a castle."

"I will kill this wicked dragon for you!" cried George, coming forward.

"I do not like to send you to fight a dragon," said the good queen. "You are very young, and you have neither horse nor armor."

"I have brought armor, a sword, a spear, and a war horse," said the princess. Then a servant brought in the armor, and it fitted George as if it had been made for him.

"Now I shall make you one of my knights," said the queen. "Be brave and true. Be watchful. Remember that a good knight must think of others before himself. When you have done your work, come back to me, so that I may thank you."

George felt so happy that he thought he could fight any number of dragons. Thanking the good queen, he set out on his journey, with Una and her servant to guide him.

When they had traveled for some hours, they came to a dark forest. Here they lost their way, and every step they took led them deeper into the woods. At last they came to a great cave. "Now I know where we are!" cried Una. "This must be the terrible Wandering Woods, in which so many travelers have died. See! There is the den of the beast that killed them!"

"Then he will kill no more!" cried George, drawing his sword. But Una begged him not to enter the cave, saying, "You will surely be killed!"

"I am a knight," answered George, walking boldly into the den. "I must not think of myself." As the great beast sprang forward, George, with one blow of the sword, struck him dead. After this, the young knight soon found the road which led out of the forest.

George and Una traveled on and on, and had many adventures. Once when George laid aside his armor to drink from a spring, a giant seized him and carried him off to a dark prison in his castle.

For three months the young knight lay in this prison, with very little food, but at last he was

rescued by another knight who was led to the giant's castle by Una. He was so weak from hunger that he had to rest and regain his strength before he could fight the dragon. So Una took George to the home of some friends who lived nearby.

When the young knight was able to walk, he went one day to see a wise old man, who surprised him greatly by saying, "Noble youth, you are the son of a king. You were stolen from your parents when you were a baby! Do not be discouraged because the giant overcame you, for you will soon be strong enough to finish the work which was given you to do. Soon you will fight a great battle and win a great victory. In the years to come, people will love and honor you for your brave deeds. They will call you, not Prince George, although your father was a king, but—Saint George."

George Kills the Dragon

The words that the wise old man spoke gave new strength to George, and soon he was able to start out again with Una to find the dragon. When they had gone some distance, they saw before them a great castle upon a hill.

"Look, Sir George!" said Una. "That is the castle in which my father and mother are shut up. The dragon must be somewhere near."

As she spoke, they heard a great roar, and the dragon rushed down the hill toward them. George raised his shield and waited, sword in hand. Then there was a terrible battle which lasted three days, but the young knight fought so bravely that at last he killed the huge beast.

George then brought Una's father and mother from the castle, telling them they need no longer be afraid. When they looked at the dead dragon and then at the young knight who had killed him, they wondered at his strength. "Thanks be to God who made you so brave, and who sent you to save us!" they cried.

People came from all over the country to look at the body of the dragon, and everyone went away praising the brave knight.

George won many battles after his fight with the dragon and became known all over the world for his goodness and his great deeds. Boys who heard the story of his bravery and his unselfishness tried to be like him, and for hundreds of years men went into battle shouting his name.

People forgot that he was a prince—they forgot where he was born—but they could never forget his goodness. And the name by which they remembered him is—"Saint George."

—*Clara E. Lynch*

MY CHICKADEE GUESTS

The air was cold, the snow was very deep, and many of the little wild birds were finding it hard to get their winter food. Some of them were dying because they could not find enough to eat. So I invited all the birds around my home to come and be my guests for the rest of the winter.

Just outside my study window I kept a tray filled with hemp, millet, and sunflower seeds, cracked nuts, and lumps of suet. There was another tray outside the bedroom window and still another outside the window of the dining room. If snow fell and covered the food in the night, I brushed it off with a whiskbroom early the next morning.

Many hungry birds came there every day to feed. There were plump pine grosbeaks, modest little redpolls, and one saucy little siskin that seemed to think he owned the whole garden.

Then there was a band of blue jays, that always acted as if they were stealing the food and were afraid of being caught at it. They did not stay to enjoy a quiet meal as the grosbeaks did, but grabbed all the food they could carry, and flew off with it. And there was an old hairy woodpecker that came for the suet. He spoke in a very loud voice and acted as if he didn't want to be interrupted.

The friendliest of all were the chickadees; they always seemed as glad to see me as I was to see them. They would come in a little flock, and if I happened to be in the garden they would alight upon my hands and shoulders, and almost ask me for something to eat.

One morning when I awoke I heard a tapping at my window pane, and there I saw four little chickadees sitting in a row on the window sill, looking into the bedroom. Snow that had fallen in the night covered all the food in the trays, and it seemed as if the little birds were trying to make me hurry with breakfast.

I decided to invite them in to have breakfast with me. I dressed quickly, went downstairs, and pulled the breakfast table close to the window. On the cloth I sprinkled broken nuts, for chickadees are very fond of nuts. Then I opened the window and whistled, and in a few moments the birds came down to the window ledge.

For a minute or two they stood peeping into the room and looking at the food on the table. Then, one after another of the little birds flew in, and snatching up the bits of nut, flew out into the garden to eat them.

Now this was very rude, for when you are invited to breakfast, you are supposed to eat at the table. So I thought I would give them a lesson in politeness. First of all I swept up the little bits of broken nuts, and then with a needle and thread I stitched several large pieces to the tablecloth.

When the chickadees came back, they tried to pick up the nuts, but they could not do it. This seemed to make them angry, for they flew out of the window and sat in the bushes nearby, scolding me.

But scolding did not make them less hungry, so back they came. By this time I was eating my

own breakfast—with an extra coat on, because the window was open. A chickadee alighted on the edge of the table and stood looking at me from under his little black cap. I sat very still, and he hopped over to half an English walnut. He tried to pick it up, but the thread held it fast.

Then he pecked at the kernel and looked up at me. I never moved, and he tried it again. He seemed to like the taste of the nut, so, holding on to the edge of the shell with his claws, he settled down and enjoyed himself.

The other chickadees looked in and saw him feeding there. One by one they followed him, until there were five birds eating breakfast with me. One of them came so near that his tail brushed my fingers. At first they were rather nervous and would fly away if I moved my hands. But they always came back, and finding that there was nothing to be afraid of, they sat at the table, or on it, rather, until they had finished.

There have been many guests at my table since that day, but few have given me more pleasure, and certainly none have been more welcome, than those little hungry chickadees.

—*Ernest Harold Baynes*

CALLING THE VIOLET

Dear little Violet,
   Don't be afraid!
Lift your blue eyes
   From the rock's mossy shade!
All the birds call for you
   Out of the sky;
May is here waiting,
   And here, too, am I.

Why do you shiver so,
   Violet sweet?
Soft is the meadow grass
   Under your feet.
Wrapped in your hood of green,
   Violet, why
Peep from your earth-door
   So silent and shy?

Trickle the little brooks
   Close to your bed;
Softest of fleecy clouds
   Float overhead;
"Ready and waiting!"
   The slender reeds sigh:
"Ready and waiting!"
   We sing—May and I.

Come, pretty Violet,
  Winter's away;
Come, for without you
  May isn't May.
Down through the sunshine
  Wings flutter and fly;
Quick, little Violet,
  Open your eye!

Hear the rain whisper,
  "Dear Violet, come!"
How can you stay
  In your underground home?
Up in the pine-boughs,
  For you the winds sigh;
Homesick to see you
  Are we—May and I.

Ha! though you care not
  For call or for shout,
Yon troop of sunbeams
  Are winning you out.
Now all is beautiful
  Under the sky;
May's here—and Violets!
  Winter, good-bye!

—*Lucy Larcom.*

BROTHER GREEN-COAT

Aunt Molly's Fairyland

Little Betty and Aunt Molly were resting in the little summerhouse by the pool. It was a warm day in early spring. Little white clouds were flying over the blue sky, just as if they were playing follow-my-leader.

"Look!" said Betty. "The clouds are out having a good time in the sunshine!"

The leaves on the trees were fresh and green. "They look as if they had just had their faces scrubbed by some elf in Fairyland," said Betty.

For a moment, the little girl was silent. Then, looking up, she said, "Wouldn't it be nice if there really were elves and fairies, Aunt Molly? How they would enjoy this day, after the long winter! I wonder where they live in winter! I mean," she said quickly, "where they would live if there really were any."

"Are you quite sure there is no Fairyland?" asked Aunt Molly. In her eyes there was a little twinkle, which always meant something pleasant and surprising.

"Oh, Aunt Molly!" cried the little girl. "Of course I know there isn't any Fairyland!"

"Some people live in Fairyland, and never know it," said Aunt Molly. "I have a little friend who has adventures that are stranger than those the fairy tales tell about."

"Oh, do tell me about him!" cried Betty.

"The first time I saw him he was very, very small," said her aunt. "He was as black as soot and he had neither arms nor legs. He had only a big head and a long tail.

"In a few days I saw him again. His tail was longer than before, and strange to say, he had two legs. The next time we met, he was bigger still, and had arms as well as legs, but his long tail was gone. The last time I saw him, he was more than a hundred times as big as at first, and he wasn't black at all; he was green and white."

Betty was puzzled. "Of course he isn't a fairy," she said. "Where did you see him, Aunt Molly?"

"All summer long he plays near this very summerhouse," said her aunt. "A little while ago, you wondered where the fairies live in winter. Well, this little friend of mine goes to a home underground to spend the winter. He stays there till days like this come again."

"Days like this! " cried Betty. "Have you seen him today, Aunt Molly? Tell me what he is like!"

"Yes, I saw him just a moment ago. He is wearing a bright green coat, and his trousers are as white and clean as if he had never lived underground. I call him Brother Green-Coat. There! I can see him now!"

BROTHER GREEN-COAT

Betty sat up quickly and looked about her. On each side of the little summerhouse, tall elms stretched out their arms. A robin was calling from one of the trees, "Cheer-up! Cheer-up! Cheer-up!" and a blue jay answered crossly," Ca-a-an't! Ca-a-an't! Ca-a-an't!"

"I know it isn't the robin," said Betty. "A robin hasn't a green coat, and he doesn't live underground in winter; he flies south. And it can't be the blue jay either; I've seen that blue jay all winter long. Did you ever speak to Brother Green-Coat, Aunt Molly? What did you say to him, and oh! did he say anything to you?"

"The strange thing about Brother Green-Coat," said Aunt Molly, "is that he never speaks when he wears black. But when he puts on his coat of green, he talks, and even sings. I have learned a little of his strange language.

"I know that he sometimes tells me that he is happy and contented; that he likes the warm air; and that he intends to go soon for a swim in the pool. But when he tells me this, it sounds just like 'Brek-kek-kek-kek! Brek-kek-kek-kek!'"

Betty was looking out over the pool. There on a dead tree, which had fallen into the water, sat a bright-eyed little creature in a coat of green, with trousers of white. He puffed himself out until he looked as if he would burst and called, "Brek-kek-kek-kek! Brek-kek-kek-kek!" in answer to Aunt Molly.

"You mean the frog! Brother Green-Coat is a frog!" cried Betty. "But you said you saw him once when he was as black as soot! How can that be? Frogs are always green."

"Did you never see the little black tadpoles wriggling about in the pool?" asked her aunt. "Before Brother Green-Coat puts on his green and white suit, he is a big tadpole, with arms and legs and a long tail; and before that, he is a very tiny tadpole, all head and tail, and as black as soot."

"And has he really a home underground?" asked the little girl, eagerly.

"When winter comes, he lives in a snug home deep in the mud at the bottom of the pool. But even in the darkness he knows when spring has come. Then he leaves his winter home to welcome the bright sunlight."

"How clean he is!" said Betty. "He doesn't look as if he had spent the winter in the mud."

"I haven't told you all about him yet," said Aunt Molly. "Come with me to the dead tree by the pool. I think we may find something there that looks as Brother Green-Coat did the very first time I saw him."

Yes! There, floating on the water, was something that looked like clear, whitish jelly, full of little black dots.

"The dots are frogs' eggs," said Aunt Molly. "The little tadpoles are hatched from them."

"And big Brother Green-Coat was once only a tiny black dot!" laughed Betty. "There! he has jumped into the pool. No wonder his green coat is so bright, and his white trousers are so clean. He washes them whenever he goes for a swim."

"Good-bye, Brother Green-Coat!" she called, as she and her aunt turned to go home. "You are just as wonderful as anything in Fairyland! I know what you mean now, Aunt Molly," she said, suddenly. "There is a Fairyland after all, and I never knew it before!"

—*Sarah A. Haste*

THE SCARECROW

The farmer looked at his cherry tree,
　　With thick buds clustered on every bough;
"I wish I could beat the Robins," said he,
　　"If somebody would only show me how!

"I'll make a terrible scarecrow grim,
　　With threatening arms and with bristling head,
And up in the trees I'll fasten him
　　To frighten them half to death," he said.

He fashioned a scarecrow, tattered and torn—
　　Oh! 'twas a horrible thing to see!
And very early, one summer morn,
　　He set it up in his cherry tree.

The blossoms were white as the light sea foam;
　　The beautiful tree was a lovely sight;
But the scarecrow stood there so much at home
　　All the birds flew screaming away in a fright.

The Robins, who watched him every day,
Heads held aslant, keen eyes so bright!
Surveying the monster began to say,
"Why should this monster our prospects blight?

"He never moves round for the roughest weather,
He's a harmless, comical, tough old fellow;
Let's all go into the tree together,
For he won't budge till the fruit is mellow!"

So up they flew, and the sauciest pair
'Mid the shady branches peered and perked,
Selected a spot with the utmost care,
And all day merrily sang and worked.

And where do you think they built their nest?
In the scarecrow's pocket, if you please.
That, half-concealed on his ragged breast,
Made a charming covert of safety and ease.

By the time the cherries were ruby red,
A thriving family, hungry and brisk,
The whole day long on the ripe fruit fed,
'Twas so convenient! They ran no risk!

—*Celia Thaxter*

WHAT KEPT THE CHIMNEY WAITING

A new brick chimney was about to be built on grandfather's house, and the boys were greatly excited over it.

"Mike's coming to mix the mortar and carry it up the ladder to the bricklayer," said Frank. "He'll tell us stories at noontimes!"

"Yes," said Walter; "and I say, Frank, let's get his hod and play we're hodcarriers, with mud for mortar. Come on!"

"Come on!" shouted Frank. "It's leaning up against the barn where he left it when he brought the things over."

On the way to the barn they saw grandfather harnessing Old Molly to the big cart. That meant a fine jolty ride down to the orchard, and the boys forgot all about playing hodcarrier, as they climbed in and jolted away.

"Mike's coming tomorrow, Grandfather, and the bricklayer, too," said Walter.

But grandfather shook his white head. "Not tomorrow, boys; you will have to wait a little longer. I sent word to the bricklayer and to Mike last night,

not to come for a few weeks yet. I have decided to put off building the new chimney."

Disappointment showed plainly in the little brown faces of the boys. What could it mean?

Grandfather did not speak again at once, for at that moment he saw a little crippled butterfly, which lay fluttering in the wheel track. Carefully he turned Old Molly, and drove to the side of the road, until the cart had passed the butterfly. For grandfather's big heart was so kind that it had room enough in it for every living creature.

Then he turned to the boys and said, "When we get home I will show you why we ought to wait before we start to build the new chimney. You will agree with me, I know. A little bird told me a great secret." And grandfather's eyes twinkled under his gray brows.

That was all the boys found out until they reached home. Then the same little bird told them the secret, too. For, without explaining the reason, grandfather took the boys up to the attic.

The old chimney had been partly torn down, half-way to the attic floor. Grandfather tiptoed up to it, and lifted the boys, one at a time, so that they could see what was inside.

"Sh!" he whispered in a soft voice. "What do you see?"

There, on a little nest of mud, lined with thistle-down and straws, sat a little bird! She blinked her bright eyes at the kind faces looking down, as if to say, "I am not afraid of you! Isn't this a beautiful nest? It is so quiet and safe! There are four speckly, freckly eggs under me. When I have hatched them, and brought up my family, then you may build your chimney, but not before."

And that was why grandfather's new chimney had to wait.

—*Annie H. Donnell*

NEST EGGS

Birds all the sunny day
  Flutter and quarrel
Here in the arbor-like
  Tent of the laurel.

Here in the fork
  The brown nest is seated;
Four little blue eggs
  The mother keeps heated.

Soon the frail eggs they shall
  Chip, and upspringing,
Make all the April woods
  Merry with singing.

Younger than we are,
  O children, and frailer,
Soon in blue air they'll be,
  Singer and sailor.

We, so much older,
  Taller, and stronger,
We shall look down on the
  Birdies no longer.

They shall go flying
  With musical speeches
High overhead in the
  Tops of the beeches.

In spite of our wisdom
  And sensible talking,
We on our feet must go
  Plodding and walking.

—Robert Louis Stevenson

ROBIN REDBREAST

Good-bye, good-bye to summer!
  For summer's nearly done;
The garden smiling faintly,
  Cool breezes in the sun;
Our thrushes now are silent,
  Our swallows flown away—
But Robin's here, in coat of brown
  And ruddy breast-knot gay.
    Robin, Robin Redbreast,
      O Robin dear!
Robin sings so sweetly
  In the falling of the year.

Bright yellow, red, and orange,
   The leaves come down in hosts;
The trees are Indian princes,
   But soon they'll turn to ghosts;
The leathery pears and apples
   Hang russet on the bough;
It's autumn, autumn, autumn late;
   'Twill soon be winter now.
     Robin, Robin Redbreast,
      O Robin dear!
And what will this poor Robin do?
   For pinching days are near.

—William Allingham

THE SHELL

I found a shell upon the shore,
I held it to my ear;
I listened gladly, while it sang
A sea song, sweet and clear.

And that a little shell could sing,
At first seemed strange to me,
Until I thought that it had learned
The music of the sea.

FRANCES KERR COOK.

I could but wish the song had words,
For then my little shell
The secrets of the deep blue sea,
To me would surely tell.

For I had wondered many times
What 'twas the water said,
When it came rushing to the shore
In waves high as my head.

But never would the little shell
Tell anything to me;
Although it sang, it still would keep
The secrets of the sea.

—*Rebecca B. Foresman*

JACK FROST AND THE PITCHER

Careless Katrina

It was a winter night—still, bright, and cold. The wagon wheels creaked loudly as they ground into the crisp snow. Even the great moon looked frosty and cold.

Katrina stood by the sitting-room window, looking out. "It is going to be a freezing night," said her father, stirring the fire. "It is growing colder every minute."

"Is it?" said her mother. "Then, Katrina, you must run upstairs and empty the china pitcher in the spare room."

"All right, Mother," said the little girl. But she was so much interested in looking out at the moonlight, that she did not move a step. Her mother was rocking the baby to sleep and she did not say anything more just then.

Fifteen minutes went by, and then mother spoke again. "Come, Katrina, go upstairs and empty the pitcher. It was Grandmother's Christmas present, and we should not like to have it broken."

"Yes, Mother, I will go in a minute."

"Well, dear, be sure to remember," said her mother, as she went off to put the baby into her crib. At that moment, in came Jamie with a pair of shining new skates, and as soon as Katrina saw them, she forgot all about the pitcher.

Just outside the window stood Jack Frost, listening and watching. When he heard Katrina say, "I will go in a minute," he chuckled and snapped his icy fingers.

"That little girl will never empty the pitcher," he said to himself; "she's one of the careless kind. Oh, I know all about careless children. Let me see— the spare room—that's for company. I'll spend the night in it! I wonder where it is."

Jack Frost knew better than to try to get into the cozy sitting room, where the bright fire was gleaming. So he slipped softly around the house, and peeped in through the kitchen window. Inside, was a stove glowing with red-hot coals.

"That is no place for me," he said, shaking his head. "The heat in there would kill me in a minute; I must look farther."

So Jack Frost went on, peeping in one window after another, until at last he saw a room that had

no fire in it. "Ah!" he whispered, "this must be the place. Yes! that is the very pitcher for me to break; and here is a fine crack for me to go through! "

Then, shaking the little frost-flakes from his long white beard, he quickly slipped into the room, and looked around.

Jack Frost's Mischief

"What a pretty room this is!" said Jack Frost. "It does seem a pity, though, to spoil such a hand-some pitcher; but, then, Katrina should not have left the water in it."

Very noiselessly Jack Frost crept along, chilling everything he touched. Soon he reached the wash-stand. Up the stand he went, nearer and nearer to the pitcher, until he could look down into it. "Not much water," he whispered as he spread his icy fingers over it. "But I can make it do."

The water in the pitcher shivered, but the icy fingers pressed down hard upon it. "Oh!" cried the water, "I am so cold! "Very soon it cried out, "If you don't go away, Jack Frost, I shall certainly freeze!"

"Good!" laughed Jack Frost. "That is just what I want you to do. I'll teach careless Katrina a lesson that she will not forget very soon."

At that very moment, Jack Frost pushed his fingers straight down into the water, and the water began to freeze. Then such a wonderful thing happened! The drops began to push and crowd against each other! Soon they pushed so hard against the sides of the pitcher that it cried out, "Drops, please stop pushing me! I am afraid that I shall break."

"We can't stop!" said the drops. "We are freezing, and we must have more room." And they kept on pushing against the sides of the poor pitcher harder than ever.

Again the pitcher groaned and called out, "Don't! Don't! I can't stand it!" But its words had no effect. The drops kept on repeating, "We must have more room! We must have more room!" And they pushed so hard that at last, with a loud cry, the poor pitcher cracked, and broke into several pieces.

When Jack Frost saw that there was nothing more for him to break, he stole softly away through the crack in the window. Just outside was old North Wind, whistling and rattling the front door. Jack Frost told him about the broken pitcher, and away they went together, laughing at the joke that had been played upon careless little Katrina.

All this time, Katrina lay dreaming in her snug little bed upstairs. She dreamed that Grandmother's pitcher was dancing gaily on the bed, and that it was beginning to glide far away on brother Jamie's new skates.

—Mary Howliston—Adapted

SIGNS OF THE SEASONS

What does it mean when the bluebird flies
  Over the hills, singing sweet and clear?
When violets peep through the blades of grass?
  These are the signs that spring is here.

What does it mean when berries are ripe?
  When butterflies flit, and honey bees hum?
When cattle stand under the shady trees?
  These are the signs that summer has come.

What does it mean when crickets chirp?
  And away to the Southland the wild geese steer?
When apples are falling, and nuts are brown?
  These are the signs that autumn is here.

What does it mean when the days are short?
  When the leaves are gone and the brooks are
    dumb?
When the fields are white with the drifting snow?
  These are the signs that winter has come.

—M. E. N. Hathaway

MOTHER SPIDER

It was a beautiful day in midsummer. The meadow was alive with busy little people moving about in the bright sunlight. A long line of ants came crawling down the path, carrying food to their home under the elm tree. Hopping along through the grass came an old toad, blinking in the warm sun.

Just a little higher up, the bees were buzzing as they flew from flower to flower. And above them all, in the clear blue sky, a robin was calling to his mate.

After a while Mother Spider came hurrying down the path, holding in her mouth a little white bag. Just then a big black beetle came rushing along the path. As Mother Spider was going in front of Mr. Toad, the beetle bumped against her and knocked the bag out of her mouth.

In an instant Mother Spider pounced angrily upon him. Though she was much smaller than the beetle, she tumbled him over upon his back. Then Mother Spider quickly took up her bag and hurried away through the grass.

"Well, I never!" said Grasshopper Green, who was playing seesaw on a blade of grass.

"I didn't want her bag," grumbled Mr. Beetle, as he wriggled to his feet. "She needn't have made such a fuss just because I stumbled against her."

"She must have something very fine in that bag," said Grasshopper Green. "She was so frightened when she dropped it! I wonder what it was."

Not long after this, Grasshopper Green started out for a little exercise. Just as he reached the brook, he saw Mother Spider coming slowly toward him. She no longer carried the little white bag, but he could see that she had something on her back.

"Good morning, neighbor," called Grasshopper Green. "Can I help you carry your things?"

"Thank you very much," she said, "but they would fall off when you give your great jumps."

"They!" cried Grasshopper Green in great surprise. And then, as he came nearer, he saw that the things on Mother Spider's back were wee baby spiders.

"Aren't they beautiful children?" the proud mother asked. "I was so afraid that something would happen to my eggs, that I never let go of the bag they were in, except once, when that stupid Mr. Beetle knocked it out of my mouth."

"Oho!" said Grasshopper Green. "So that was what frightened you, was it? That bag was full of eggs! And now you are carrying all those children on your back. Doesn't it tire you?"

"I don't mind the weight," said Mother Spider, "if only the children are well and safe. In a little while, you know, they will be able to run about by themselves. Then we shall be very happy here in the meadow grass. Oh, a family like this is well worth the trouble, neighbor."

"Yes," said Grasshopper Green, "I have a dozen wee boys of my own at home. And that reminds me that it is time to go home to breakfast! Good-bye, Neighbor Spider."

So home he went. And happy Mother Spider kept on her way to find a breakfast for the babies she loved so well.

—*Frances Bliss Gillespy*

A SONG OF JOY

The robin sings of willow buds,
Of snow-flakes on the green;
The bluebird sings of mayflowers,
The fallen leaves between;
The wee wren has a thousand tales
To tell to girl and boy;
But the oriole, the oriole,
Sings, "Joy! joy! joy!"

The pewee calls his little mate,
When she is far away;
The warbler sings, "What fun, what fun,
To tilt upon the spray!"
The cuckoo has no song, but clucks,
Just like a wooden toy;
But the oriole, the oriole,
Sings, "Joy! joy! joy!"

—*Laura E. Richards*

THE SLEEPING BEAUTY

THE WICKED FAIRY

Once upon a time there lived a king and a queen who for many years were very sad because they had no child. At last a little daughter came to them, and the king was so happy that he gave a great feast in the palace and invited all his friends.

Now in his country there were thirteen fairies. Of course the king wished to invite all of these fairies to the feast, so that each might give his dear child a fairy gift.

"How can you invite them all?" asked the queen. "We have only twelve golden plates. One of the fairies must stay at home."

So twelve of the fairies were invited, and a wonderful feast was given at the palace. When it came to an end, the fairies gave their magic gifts to the baby. One said to the child, "You shall be good." Another said, "You shall be wise." A third gave her beauty, and a fourth, riches; and so on with everything in the world that one could wish for.

When eleven of the fairies had named their gifts, and just as the twelfth was about to speak, in walked

the thirteenth fairy. She was very angry because she had not been invited to the feast. Without even looking at anyone, she cried with a loud voice, "When the princess is fifteen years of age, she shall prick herself with a spindle, and shall fall dead!"

Everyone was frightened at this; but the twelfth fairy had not yet told what her gift would be. As soon as the wicked fairy had finished speaking, she came forward and said, "The king's daughter shall not die. A deep sleep will fall upon her, but she will awake at the end of a hundred years."

From that time on, the king and queen were very sad. "How can I keep my dear child from this sad fate?" the king asked himself over and over. One day the thought came to him, "Surely my daugh-

ter cannot touch a spindle if she never sees one."
So he gave orders that every spindle in the whole
country should be burned. But an old woman who
lived in the tower of the palace hid her spindle.
"No one shall burn it," she said. "It will be safe in
my room in the tower."

As time passed, the fairy gifts came to the young
princess. She grew to be good and gentle and wise
and beautiful. Everyone who saw her loved her.

On the day when she became fifteen years old, it
happened that the king and queen were suddenly
called away from home. The maiden was left in
the palace quite alone, so she went about, looking
into all sorts of places, in room after room, just as
she liked.

At last she came to the tower of the palace. Up
the narrow, winding staircase she climbed until
she reached a little door. A rusty key was in the
lock, and when she turned it, the door sprang
open. There in a little room sat an old woman with
a spindle, busily spinning flax.

"Good morning!" said the princess, entering the
room. "What are you doing?"

"I am spinning," said the old woman.

"What sort of thing is this, that spins around so merrily?" asked the princess, as she took the spindle in her hand and tried to spin.

But hardly had she given the wheel a single turn, when the words of the wicked fairy came true. For the beautiful princess pricked her finger upon the spindle, and at that very moment sank back upon a bed that stood near, and lay in a deep sleep.

And this sleep fell upon all in the palace. The king and queen, who had just come home, fell asleep. The servants fell into the same deep sleep. The horses went to sleep in the stables, the pigeons upon the roof of the palace, and the flies upon the wall.

Even the fire that was flaming on the hearth became quiet, and slept. The meat stopped roasting. The cook, who was just about to scold the kitchen boy because he had forgotten something, suddenly fell asleep. At the same moment, the wind became still, and on the great trees in front of the castle not a leaf moved again.

Then round about the castle there began to grow a hedge of thorns, which became higher every year. At last nothing could be seen of the castle, not even the flag on the tower.

The Young Prince

A hundred years went by. Then it happened that a young prince came to that country and heard the story of the enchanted castle. When he heard how the poor princess and all the household slept under the spell of the angry fairy, he cried, "I will find this Sleeping Beauty and wake her!"

The next day he set out for the castle. When he came to the place where the thorn-hedge had been, he found nothing but flowers, which instantly opened a pathway for him.

In the castle-yard he saw the horses lying asleep. On the roof sat the pigeons with their heads under their wings. When he entered the house, the flies were asleep upon the wall. The cook in the kitchen was still pointing her finger at the forgetful boy. Inside the castle, the king and queen slept upon their thrones. The lords and ladies of their palace sat about them, slumbering peacefully.

The prince went on from room to room, and at last came to the tower where the princess was sleeping. So beautiful did she look that he stooped and kissed her. At his touch the princess opened her eyes and smiled at him.

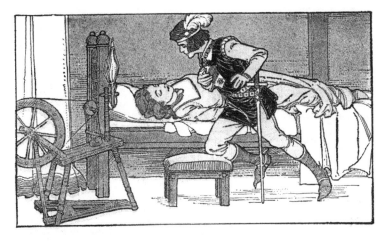

Together they went down and awoke the king and the queen. Then all the people in the castle awoke and looked at each other in great surprise.

The horses in the stables stood up and shook themselves. The pigeons on the roof raised their heads from under their wings, looked around, and flew into the country. The flies buzzed and flew from the walls. The fire in the kitchen roasted the meat, and the cook shook her finger and scolded the forgetful boy.

Then the prince married the princess, with feasting and rejoicing, and they lived happily ever after.

—Grimm

CINDERELLA, OR
THE LITTLE GLASS SLIPPER

CINDERELLA'S SELFISH SISTERS

Once upon a time there was a proud, selfish woman who had three daughters. The two older girls were proud and selfish, too, but the other daughter was kind and good.

Now this unkind woman loved her two selfish daughters greatly, because they were so much like herself, but she had no love in her heart for the youngest daughter. It always made her angry to hear the neighbors praise the kind and gentle manners of the youngest girl.

So the mother gave her the hardest work in the house to do; she had to scour the dishes and the tables, scrub the floors, and clean the bedrooms.

She slept in the attic upon a hard straw bed, while her two sisters had fine rooms and the very softest beds. They had looking glasses, too, so large that they could see themselves at full length.

The poor girl bore her hard life patiently. She did not complain to her father, because she knew that he would scold her if she said anything against her mother. For the selfish woman made him believe that she was right in all things.

When the tired girl had finished her work, she often went into the chimney corner and sat down there among the cinders. Because of this habit, she came to be called Cinder-girl. The younger of the two favorite sisters, who was not quite so rude as the older, called her Cinderella.

Cinderella, in spite of the poor clothes that she had to wear, was a hundred times more beautiful than either of her sisters. Even her mother knew this, and the thought of it made her very angry.

Now it happened that the king's son gave a ball, and Cinderella's two sisters were invited to it. Of course they were much pleased at the honor, and for the next few days they were busy choosing the gowns they were to wear. All day long the selfish girls talked of nothing but how they should be dressed when they went to the ball.

"For my part," said the older, "I shall wear my red velvet gown with pearl trimmings. It is the most beautiful of all my dresses."

"And I," said the younger, "shall wear my pink satin dress. I shall put on my gold-flowered cloak, too, and wear all my diamonds."

Cinderella was now obliged to work harder than ever, for it was she who ironed her sisters' clothes. She helped them to get ready for the ball in every way that she could, for she was always kind, even to her selfish sisters. She told them what was best to wear, and even dressed their hair for them.

As she was doing this, one of them said to her, "Cinderella, would you like to go to the ball?"

"Oh, sister!" she answered, "a girl like me could not go to a ball!"

"You are right," said the other sister; "people would laugh to see a Cinder-girl at a ball."

At last the happy evening came. As Cinderella watched her two sisters drive off to the palace, she could not keep the tears from her eyes, at the thought that she could not go with them.

The Fairy Godmother

Now Cinderella had a godmother who was a fairy. When the godmother saw the young girl in tears, she asked what troubled her.

"I wish I could—I wish I could—" but Cinderella was sobbing so hard that she could not tell what made her sad.

As her godmother was a fairy, she could guess what was in the girl's mind. So she said to her, "You wish you could go to the ball, do you not?"

"Alas, yes," said Cinderella, sighing.

"Well," said the godmother, "be a good girl, and I will see that you go. Run out into the garden and bring me the largest pumpkin you can find there."

Cinderella went at once and brought a fine pumpkin to her godmother, but she could not think how it would help her to go to the ball. She was still more puzzled when she saw her godmother scoop out all the inside of it, leaving nothing but the rind. Then the fairy struck it with her wand, and instantly the pumpkin was turned into the most wonderful coach that Cinderella had ever seen in all her life.

"How shall we get horses for such a great coach as this, Godmother?" asked Cinderella.

"In the corner of the kitchen," said the fairy, "you will find a mousetrap; bring it to me."

Cinderella went to look for the mousetrap, and when she found it, she saw in it six mice, all alive. Wondering what her godmother meant by her strange request, Cinderella brought the trap to the fairy.

Then the godmother opened the door of the trap and gave each mouse, as it went out, a little tap with her wand. At the touch, each mouse was turned into a beautiful horse. The six mice made a fine team of six large white horses.

"Wonderful!" cried Cinderella, joyfully. "But, Godmother, we have no coachman. I will see if there is not a rat in the rattrap—you might make a coachman of him."

"You are right," replied her godmother. "Bring the trap to me."

So Cinderella brought the rattrap to her, and in it were three large rats. The fairy chose the rat that had the longest beard and touched him with her wand. Instantly he was turned into a fat coachman.

Then the fairy godmother said, "Go into the garden and you will find six lizards behind the watering pot; bring them to me."

The happy girl had no sooner brought the lizards, than her godmother turned them into six footmen. They jumped upon the back of the coach and held on as if they had done nothing else all their lives. The fairy then said to Cinderella, "Well, you see here a coach fit to go to the ball in; are you not pleased with it?"

"Yes, yes!" cried Cinderella; "but shall I go as I am, in these rags?"

Then the fairy godmother touched Cinderella with the wand, and her clothes were turned into cloth of gold and silver, all shining with jewels. On her feet were a pair of wonderful glass slippers. Cinderella climbed into the beautiful coach and sat down. Never in her life had she been so happy!

"Now, remember one thing," said her godmother; "do not stay after midnight. For if you stay one moment after the clock strikes twelve, the coach will be turned to a pumpkin again, the horses will be turned to mice, the coachman will become a rat, the footmen will all be lizards, and your pretty clothes will become rags."

Cinderella promised her godmother that she would surely leave the ball before midnight. Then she drove joyfully away in the wonderful coach.

CINDERELLA AT THE BALL

When Cinderella reached the palace, the king's son was told that a princess whom nobody knew had come to the ball. As she stepped from the coach, he ran out to greet her, and led her into the great ballroom.

At once everyone stopped dancing; nothing was heard but a murmur of voices saying, "Ah! how beautiful she is! Ah! how beautiful she is!" The king himself could not keep his eyes away from her, and the queen said that it had been a long time since she had seen so lovely a girl.

All the ladies at the ball began to look carefully at the clothes of the unknown princess, so that they might have some made just like them.

The king's son led Cinderella to the seat of honor and afterwards took her out to dance with him. So gracefully did she dance that everyone admired her more and more. When the great supper was served, the young prince could not eat. He did nothing but bring dainty food to the unknown princess, and sit looking at her beautiful face.

Cinderella sat down beside her sisters and was very kind to them, giving them some of the oranges and cakes that the prince had brought her. This kindness surprised and pleased them greatly, for they did not know who she was, and they thought it a great honor to be noticed by so beautiful a princess.

In the midst of her pleasure Cinderella suddenly heard the clock strike a quarter to twelve. Without saying a word, she hastened away as fast as she could go. When she reached home, she ran to find her godmother, so that she might thank her.

"Oh, how I wish I might go to the ball tomorrow night, too!" said the young girl. "The king's son asked me to come."

As she was telling her godmother all that had happened, her two sisters entered the room. "How long you have stayed!" said Cinderella, yawning, rubbing her eyes, and stretching herself as if she had just awakened.

"If you had been at the ball," said one of the sisters, "you would not be tired or sleepy. The most beautiful princess that ever was seen came there. She was very kind to us and gave us oranges and cakes that the prince himself had given to her. It was a great honor."

Cinderella asked them the name of the princess, but of course they could not tell her. "The king's son does not know it, either," they said. "He would give all the world to know who she is."

At these words, Cinderella smiled and asked, "Was she really so very beautiful? How lucky you have been! I wish that I could see her! Ah! dear Charlotte, do lend me the yellow dress that you wear every day! Then I can go to the ball tomorrow and see the strange princess."

"No, indeed," cried Charlotte. "Lend my clothes to a Cinder-girl like you! I should not think of doing such a thing."

THE GLASS SLIPPER

The next night, after the sisters had gone to the ball, the fairy godmother sent Cinderella, too, dressed even more splendidly than before. Again the king's son was always at her side, and this pleased her so much that she quite forgot her godmother's warning about leaving before midnight. She heard the clock begin to strike twelve, when she thought that it could not be later than eleven.

Then Cinderella ran quickly from the ballroom. The prince ran after her, but he could not overtake her. As she ran, one of her glass slippers fell off, and the prince picked it up carefully.

The young girl had to run all the way home, for at the stroke of twelve the coach turned back again to a pumpkin, just as the fairy had said it would do. She had nothing left of all her fine clothes except one of the little glass slippers.

When the two sisters returned from the ball, Cinderella asked them if the princess had been there.

"Yes," said her sister Charlotte, "but she hurried away so fast when the clock struck twelve that she dropped one of her little glass slippers. The king's son picked it up and took it into the palace."

A few days afterwards, the prince sent out a messenger who called to all the people, "The king's son will marry the maiden whose foot the little glass slipper exactly fits!"

The messenger tried the wonderful slipper on all the princesses and all the ladies of the king's palace, but it was too small for them. He brought it to the two sisters, but it was too small for them, too. Then Cinderella said, "Let me try it on."

Her sisters laughed at her, but the messenger looked earnestly at the young girl, for he saw that she was very beautiful. "Try it on, fair maiden," he said; " I have orders that every lady is to try on the slipper."

So Cinderella sat down and put the slipper on her foot. How surprised her sisters were when they saw that it fitted perfectly! Their surprise was still greater when Cinderella brought out the mate to the slipper and put it on her other foot.

At that very moment the fairy godmother came into the room and touched Cinderella with her wand. Instantly the young girl was even more splendidly dressed than when she had gone to the ball.

Her sisters knew now that Cinderella was the beautiful lady whom they had seen at the palace. Throwing themselves at her feet, they begged pardon for all their unkind treatment of her. Cinderella lifted them up and put her arms aound them. With all her heart, she forgave them and begged them to love her always.

Then the messenger led her to the young prince, who thought her more charming than ever. A few days later, the king's son and the beautiful maiden were married. Cinderella, who was as good as she was beautiful, gave her two sisters a home in the palace, where they lived very happily.

—*Charles Perrault—Adapted*

FAIRYLAND

The woods are just behind our house,
 And every afternoon at four
I go to pick the lovely flowers
 That grow right up beside the door;
Nurse says that just old weeds are there—
I call them Garlands for Queen's hair.

Sometimes a queer noise in our woods
 Will frighten me when no one's by;
And if I hear it after dark
 I run away to hide and cry.
Nurse says it's just the cows I hear—
I think it's Giants creeping near.

The woods stretch westward far away,
 The trees are very tall and green;
They grow on little dimpled hills,
 With grassy hollows in between.
Nurse says our woods aren't very grand—
I think that they are *FAIRYLAND*.

       —Gwendolen Haste

HANS AND THE FOUR GREAT GIANTS

Hans Goes Out into the World

Once upon a time there lived a little boy whose name was Hans. His home was in a village where the trees shaded the green grass that grew around the houses. Hans loved his home very much. He loved to hear the birds sing and to watch them fly high in the air, and he often threw crumbs upon the ground for them to eat.

Hans was a happy little fellow, who was always busy doing something for somebody. When he became a tall, strong lad, he often went with his father into the forest to chop wood.

One day, when Hans had grown to be a young man, his father said to him, "Hans, my boy, it is time for you to start out to find some work for yourself. You must go out into the world and learn how to take care of yourself."

So his mother packed his clothes in a little bundle, and as she kissed him good-bye said, "Hans, my dear son, always be brave and true." Then he started on his journey.

Hans walked a long way until he came to a great city. Here he soon found work in the shop of a blacksmith. Every time he struck a blow with his heavy hammer, great sparks flew from the red-hot iron, and this pleased the boy very much. The work made his arms grow strong and his chest broad.

Every day Hans saw a beautiful princess drive past the blacksmith's shop. She was the most beautiful princess in the world. Hans often said to himself, "How I wish I could serve this lovely princess!"

At last one day he went to the palace gate and asked the gatekeeper if there was not some work for him to do in the palace.

"What can you do?" asked the gatekeeper.

"I am willing to do any kind of work that the king may need to have done," answered Hans.

So the keeper of the gate told the king that there was a tall young man waiting outside, who wanted to serve him.

"Bring him to me," said the king.

When Hans came before the throne, the king said, "What can you do, young man?" And again Hans replied, "I am willing to do anything that you may need to have done. Most of all, I should like to serve the beautiful princess."

"You would, would you?" cried the king. "Now I will test you. At the bottom of the North Sea there lies a string of enchanted pearls. If you will get those pearls and bring them to me, you shall serve the princess."

THE ENCHANTED PEARLS

Hans was so delighted at the thought that some-time he might serve the beautiful princess, that he turned and hastened out of the palace. The very next day he started on his journey to the North Sea. He walked and walked, until he was very tired. At last he saw a great giant rushing along toward him in the strangest manner.

"Good-morning!" said Hans. "What a large giant you are!"

"Yes," replied the giant, looking down at Hans, "I need to be both large and strong. Where are you going, young man?"

"I am going to the North Sea to get a string of enchanted pearls that lies at the bottom of the sea," answered Hans.

"Ah!" said the great giant, "it will take you a long time to get there. Now if you could walk as fast as I can, it would be an easy matter."

"How fast can you walk?" asked Hans.

"I can walk faster than the swiftest horse can run," answered the giant.

"I wish you would come with me," said Hans. "After I find the pearls, I want to get back to the king's palace as soon as possible. For if I find the necklace, I am to serve the beautiful princess."

"If that is the case," said the giant, " I think I will go along with you."

So the two walked along together, until they saw what Hans thought was a huge round stone ahead of them. But when they came to it, he saw that it was another giant, lying asleep by the roadside.

"I will cut some branches from a tree to shade that poor fellow's face," said Hans. "The sun is so hot that it will hurt his eyes."

At these words the first giant laughed aloud. "Ho, ho, ho!" he cried. "Don't you know who that is? That is a neighbor of mine. He has the strongest eyes in the world. He can see a fly on the leaf of a tree that is a mile away."

The loud laugh awoke the sleeping giant, who opened his great eyes and stared in surprise at Hans. "Why are you cutting those branches, young man?" he growled.

" Oh," said Hans, " I meant to stick them into the ground, so that they might keep the hot sun out of your eyes."

"Bah!" cried the great giant, sitting up. "Don't you know that my eyes are so strong that I can look the noonday sun straight in the face?"

"Indeed! Indeed!" said Hans. "What a wonderful giant you must be. I wish you would come with me. I need your strong eyes, for I am on my way to the North Sea, to search for a necklace of pearls that lies at the bottom of the sea."

"Oho!" said the giant; "if that's the case, I think I will go with you."

So Hans and the two great giants walked on together. They had not gone more than three or four miles, when Hans saw another giant, sitting under a tall tree. As they came up to him, the wind blew the giant's hat off his head and carried it far away.

"I will get it for you," cried Hans, as he ran after the hat. But before he could reach the spot where the hat lay, the giant stretched out his long arm, picked up his hat, and put it upon his head. At this, all three of the great giants broke into a hearty laugh.

"Young man, didn't you know that this is the giant whose arms are so long that he can reach five hundred yards?" asked the swift-footed giant.

"No!" exclaimed Hans, dancing with delight. "But if that is true, you are just the giant I need. When

I get to the North Sea, you can reach down to the bottom and pick up the necklace of pearls that I am seeking. Will you come along and help me?"

"Yes," said the long-armed giant, "I will go, if I can be of any use to you."

So Hans and the three great giants started gaily on their journey to the North Sea. They had not gone far before Hans saw in the distance still another giant, leaning up against a very large rock.

Hans noticed that both of this giant's ears were filled with cotton. "Have you the earache?" asked the boy. "Perhaps I can do something to help you."

"Oh, no," said the giant, "I always stuff cotton into my ears, to shut off some of the sounds about me. I can hear so well that I can tell what men are saying far away—even if they are a hundred miles from me."

"What a wonderful giant you must be!" said Hans. "Will you come with me? I am going in search of a necklace of pearls that lies at the bottom of the North Sea. When I get it, you can tell me whether the king is at his palace, so that I can give it to him."

"You think you will need me, do you?" said the good-natured giant. "Well, I'll go along."

HANS WINS THE PRINCESS

So Hans and the four great giants walked along until they came to the North Sea. Then they got into a boat and rowed out to the deep water. The giant who could see so far soon found the place where the necklace lay at the bottom of the sea. Then the giant whose arms were so long reached down and picked up the necklace and laid it in the boat.

Hans and the giants now rowed back to the shore. As soon as they had landed, the giant who could hear so well took the cotton out of his right ear and listened to what was being said at the king's palace. He heard the people in the palace talking of a splendid ball that was to be given the next night, in honor of the birthday of the beautiful princess.

He then told Hans what he had heard. At once the giant who could run so fast stooped down and let Hans climb up and seat himself upon his great shoulders. Away the two went, faster than a bird could fly! They reached the palace in time for Hans to give the necklace of pearls to the king, just as he was about to seat his beautiful daughter upon a throne beside his own.

So greatly was the king pleased with the necklace that he at once gave orders that Hans should serve the beautiful princess. And so faithfully did Hans serve her that she learned to love him dearly, and in time they were married. When the old king died, Hans was made king, and the beautiful princess became queen.

You may be sure that Hans took good care of his old father and mother. He also asked his four friends, the giants, to come and live in his kingdom. With their help, it became the richest country on the face of the earth. From all over the world travelers came to visit it.

—Elizabeth Harrison

THE UGLY DUCKLING

The Great Egg

The country was very beautiful, for it was summer. The wheat was yellow, the oats were green, and the hay was stacked in the meadows.

The warm sunshine fell on an old house and on the little stream that flowed near it. By the water's edge grew large burdock leaves, so tall that children could stand under them. The spot was wild and lonely, and that was the reason a duck had chosen it for her nest.

There she sat under the great burdocks, waiting for her eggs to hatch. At last the shells cracked, and the mother duck heard "tchick, tchick!" as one little head after another peeped out. "Quack, quack!" said the duck, and all the little ones stood up as well as they could, looking about under the green leaves.

"How large the world is!" said the little ones.

"You must not think that this is the whole of the world," said the mother. "It reaches far beyond the other side of the garden, to the edge of the woods; but I have never been there."

"Are you all here?" she asked, getting up. "No, all the eggs are not yet hatched; the largest egg is still in the nest. I have been sitting here a long time, and I am very tired." Then she sat down again.

"Good morning! How are you getting on?" asked a friendly old duck.

"This one egg keeps me so long!" answered the mother. "It will not break. But all the other eggs have hatched. Look at my pretty ducklings! I think they are the prettiest I have ever seen."

"Yes, they are very pretty," said the old duck. "But let me see the egg that will not break. It may be a turkey's egg. I was cheated in that way once, myself, and I had such trouble with the young one. He was so afraid of the water that I could not get him to go in. I called and scolded, but it was no use. Let me see the egg. Ah, yes! that is a turkey's egg. Leave it, and teach the other little ones to swim."

"I will sit on it a little longer," said the duck. "I have been sitting so long that I may as well stay until this last egg is hatched."

"Do as you please," said the old duck, and away she went.

In the Farmyard

The great egg broke at last. "Tchick, tchick!" said the little one, as it tumbled out of the shell. Oh, how ugly it was!

"It is not like the others; it is gray," said the mother. "Can it be a young turkey? We shall soon find out, for it must go into the water, even though I push it in myself."

The next day was fine, and the sun shone warmly upon the great burdock leaves. Mother Duck with all her family of little ducklings went down to the stream to have a swim. Plump! she went into the cool water, and called out loudly to her children, "Quack, quack!" One duckling after another jumped in and began to swim. All were there, even the ugly gray one.

"No, it is not a turkey," said the old duck. "See how well it swims! It is my own child! It is really very pretty, too, when one looks at it carefully. Quack, quack! Now come with me. I will take you to the farmyard. Keep close to me, and look out for the cat."

So they went to the farmyard, where it was very crowded and noisy. "Keep together," said the

mother duck, "and bow to the old duck yonder. She is a Spanish duck, and a great lady.

"Don't turn your feet in; a good duckling always keeps his feet far apart, just as his father and mother do. Now bow your necks and say 'Quack.'"

The ducklings did as they were told. All the other ducks looked at them and said, "Just see! Now we have another family. Were there not enough here already? And look how ugly that big one is! Let us drive him away." Then one of the ducks flew at him and bit him.

"Stop biting him!" said the mother. "He is doing no harm. Stop biting him!"

"Yes, but he is so big and ugly!" said the other ducks. "We do not like him."

"All of your children, except that big one, are very beautiful," said the Spanish duck. "He does not seem to have turned out well."

"He is not handsome," said the mother, "but he is a very good child, and he swims even better than the others. He stayed too long in the shell; that is the reason he is not like them."

The duck and her family soon made themselves at home in the farmyard. But the ugly gray duckling was bitten and pecked and teased by all the ducks and hens in the yard.

"He is so large and ugly," they all said.

Even the turkey puffed himself out and marched up to the duckling. "Gobble, gobble, gobble," he said, growing red with anger. He had spurs and thought himself king of the farmyard, from one end to the other.

The poor gray duckling was very much frightened. "I wonder why I am so ugly!" he said to himself. "No one seems to like me."

This was the first day, but afterwards things grew worse. Even his own brothers and sisters were unkind to him. The ducks bit him, and the hens pecked him. The turkey puffed and gobbled at him, and the girl who fed them pushed him away from the food.

"That is because I am so ugly," thought the poor duckling. "I must run away from this place where everyone treats me so cruelly."

So he ran through the hedge and down the road. "Oh, how ugly I must be!" he thought. For all the birds he met were frightened and flew away. At last he came to a wide marsh, where the wild ducks lived. Here he lay a whole night, tired and lonely.

In the morning the wild ducks flew up and saw the duckling. "Who are you?" they asked. The duckling did not answer, but he bowed as politely as he could.

"You are very ugly," they all cried. "But that does not matter to us, for we shall not see you again." And away they all flew.

At that moment the ugly duckling happened to turn his head. There stood a great dog, that opened his jaws and showed his teeth. Then, splash! he was gone.

"Well! let me be thankful," sighed the duckling, as he ran away from the marsh. "I am so ugly that even a hungry dog will not eat me."

In the Hut

As night came on, the ugly gray duckling looked around for a place to sleep and at last saw a little hut. The door of the but was open, so the duckling crept through, into a room. There he hid himself in a corner and went to sleep.

In this hut lived an old woman with her cat and hen. The cat knew how to hump up his back and purr. The hen knew how to lay very good eggs, and the old woman loved her dearly.

The next morning the cat and the hen saw the ugly gray duckling. The cat began to mew and the hen to cackle.

"What is the matter?" asked the old woman, looking around. She could not see very well, so she thought that the ugly duckling was a fat duck that had lost her way. "This is a good catch," she said to herself. "I shall now have duck's eggs whenever I want them." So the duckling was allowed to stay for three weeks, but not a single duck's egg was laid in the hut.

Now the cat was master of the house, and the hen was mistress. They thought that they were very handsome and very clever. The duckling did not agree with them, but the hen would not allow him to say so.

"Can you lay eggs?" the hen asked the ugly duckling, one day.

"No," answered the poor duckling.

"Well, then, hold your tongue."

Next, the cat went up to him and said, "Can you hump up your back? Can you purr?"

"No," answered the ugly duckling, again.

"Then keep still when sensible persons are speaking to you."

So the duckling sat alone in a corner of the hut and felt very sad. After a while he happened to think of the fresh air and the warm sunshine, and he wished very much that he could have a swim. He could not help telling the hen about his wish.

"The trouble with you," said the hen, "is that you have nothing to do. That is why you have these strange thoughts. Either lay eggs, or purr; then you will not have such thoughts."

"But it is so pleasant to swim," said the duckling. "Oh, how fine it is when the water closes over your head, and you plunge straight down to the bottom of the pond!"

"Well! that is a queer sort of pleasure!" said the hen. "I think you must be crazy. Do you think I should like to swim, or to plunge to the bottom of the water? Ask the cat if he would like it; he is sensible. Ask the old woman; there is no one in the world wiser than she is. Do you think she would like to have the water closing over her head?"

"You do not understand me," said the duckling. "I mean that I like to dive."

"What! We do not understand you!" cried the hen. "Do you think that you are wiser than we are? Be thankful for our kindness. You have a warm room, and you can learn something from us. Come! Take the trouble to learn to purr or to lay eggs."

"No," said the duckling, sadly, "I think I will go out into the wide world again."

So the duckling went to look for a new home. He walked a long way, until he came to a great lake. How glad he was to swim upon the water and to plunge his head beneath it! But he still was very lonely, for all the birds passed by and would have nothing to do with him because he was so ugly.

THE BEAUTIFUL SWAN

Month after month the ugly duckling swam upon the clear water of the great lake. By and by autumn came, the leaves turned brown, and the wind whirled them about. The air was cold, and the clouds were heavy with snow. The poor duckling was cold and lonely and unhappy.

One evening just at sunset, a flock of large, beautiful birds rose out of the reeds. Never before had the duckling seen anything so beautiful. Their feathers were as white as snow, and they had long, slender necks, for they were swans. With a strange, wild cry, they spread their long, splendid wings, and flew away. They were leaving the cold lake and going to warm countries across the open sea.

They flew so high, so very high! The ugly duckling stretched his neck to look after the beautiful birds as they flew away. Then he called to them, for he could not help it. It was a loud, strange cry that he gave; it frightened him to hear it.

From that time on, he felt more lonely than ever. He did not know what kind of birds they were; he did not know where they were flying; but he knew that he loved them. He had never loved anything in all his life as he loved those great, beautiful birds, with their splendid wings. Still he did not dare to wish for such beauty as they had.

"I am so ugly that I can never be beautiful," he said to himself. "Even the ducks will not let me stay with them."

All through the long winter, the duckling was unhappy. It was so cold, so very cold! He had to swim round and round in the water to keep from freezing. It would make you sad to hear all that he suffered.

Then, after a long time, a warm day came. The sun shone brightly, and the birds sang happily. Beautiful spring had come. The duckling lay on the edge of the lake among the reeds. The warm sunshine filled him with so much joy that he shook his wings. They were stronger than they had ever been before; to his great surprise, he found that they bore him up in the air and carried him away.

Soon he came to a large garden, where the apple trees were in full bloom. Oh, everything was so lovely! The garden was full of the freshness of spring. The apple trees bent over a stream, and their blossoms looked at themselves in the water.

Then out of a thicket nearby came three beautiful swans. They seemed very proud of their white feathers that gleamed in the sunshine as they swam lightly, oh, so lightly on the stream. The graceful birds curved their slender necks and looked at themselves in the water. The lonely duckling had seen them in the autumn, and here they were again.

"I will fly to those wonderful birds!" he said to himself. "They may kill me because I am so ugly, but I do not care. It would be better to be killed by them than to suffer during another long, cold, lonely winter."

So the duckling flew into the water and swam toward the beautiful swans. When they saw him, they turned and came swimming to meet him.

"Kill me, beautiful birds, for I am so ugly and so lonely that I do not wish to live!" said the poor duckling, as he bowed his head.

But when he looked down, what was it that he saw in the water! It was the image of himself. He was no longer gray and ugly; he was a beautiful swan, with shining feathers as white as snow!

Some little children who were playing in the garden threw bread into the water for the swans. "Look, look!" cried the youngest child. "There is a new swan!" And all the other children clapped their hands and danced and cried out, "Yes, there is a new swan! How beautiful he is!"

The young swan hid his head under his wing, for he was so happy that he did not know what to do.

He was almost too happy, but he was not proud. He remembered how he had been laughed at and pecked and bitten. Now he heard everyone say that he was the most beautiful of all the birds. "When I was the ugly duckling," he said to himself, "I did not dream that I could ever be so happy!"

—Hans Christian Andersen

VACATION TIME

Good-bye, little desk at school, good-bye,
We're off to the fields and the open sky.
The bells of the brooks and the woodland bells
Are ringing us out to the vales and dells,
To meadow-ways fair, and to hill-tops cool,
Good-bye, little desk at school.

Good-bye, little desk at school, good-bye,
We've other brave lessons and tasks to try;
But we shall come back in the fall, you know,
And as gay to come as we are to go,
With ever a laugh and never a sigh
Good-bye, little desk, good-bye!

—Frank Hutt

HELPS TO STUDY

Suppose some evening, just before bedtime, that your mother said to you, "Tonight I am going to tell you a story that is hundreds and hundreds of years old. It is so interesting that mothers all over the world have told it to their children ever since the world was young." Wouldn't you be eager to hear it?

Well, the first part of this reader—"Fables and Folk Tales"—is made up of just that kind of stories. Some of them, called fables, are very short and teach a useful lesson in a funny way. Thousands of years ago a slave in a country called Greece made a collection of these little stories. His name was Aesop, and his fables were so amusing that they have been remembered ever since. When you have read the two fables by Aesop that are given in this part of your book, tell the class which was the more interesting to you.

Some of the longer stories in this group are called folk tales, because they have been told by the folks of different countries for so many years that no one knows who first made them up. Some of them will give you a good laugh, and others will show how foolish it is to brag or to wish for things that you cannot get. When you have read all of them, tell the class which story seemed the funniest, and which one teaches the best lesson.

After you have read each fable or folk tale, see if you can answer all the questions that you will find on the following pages.

The Hare and the Hedgehog, p. 9. 1. Why did the hedgehog think the hares were rude? 2. What did the hare say that made the little hedgehog angry? 3. Read the reply of the hedgehog. 4. The hedgehog thought the hare was too proud of his long legs; what did he say he would teach the hare? 5. What word do we sometimes use instead of "boast"? 6. Tell the story of the joke that the hedgehogs played on the hare. 7. What did the little hedgehog mean when he said, "Brains are better than legs"? 8. This story is a "folk tale"; can you see why folks in different countries told it over and over?

Old Horses Know Best, p. 15. 1. What were the two horses doing? 2. Why did the old horse go down the hill slowly? 3. What happened to the young horse and his cart? 4. Do you know what "ruts" are? 5. What did the young horse learn from the accident? 6. Did you ever get into trouble because you thought you knew better than some older person?

The Miser, p. 16. 1. What is a miser? 2. Where did the miser hide his gold? 3. What happened to it? 4. What question did the neighbor ask the miser? 5. Do you think it would do the miser as much good to look at the hole as to look at the gold? 6. This is one of Aesop's fables; who was Aesop? What is a fable? 7. Dramatize (act as a play) the story, using for some of the speeches, the same words the people say in the fable.

The Dog and the Horse, p. 17. 1. What did the neighbors say about Stefan's farm? Can you use another word instead of "autumn"? 2. Read the dog's speech to the horse. 3. Read the reply of the horse. 4. Why did the dog have nothing to say? 5. Which do you think is the more helpful to the farmer, the dog or the horse? 6. What mistake did the dog make?

The Fox and the Crow, p. 18. 1. What plan had the fox for getting the cheese? 2. Did the plan work well? 3. What did the crow learn when it was too late to save the cheese? 4. Tell the story in your own words. 5. This is another of Aesop's fables; what lesson did Aesop intend to teach in it?

Why the Rabbit's Tail Is Short, p. 20. 1. Why did the rabbit wish to cross the swamp? 2. What reason did the rabbit give for thinking that the alligator was too proud to carry him across the swamp? 3. Find lines that show why the rabbit is called "sly." 4. Read the rabbit's boastful words after he got across the swamp. 5. What shows that the rabbit laughed too soon? 6. Tell the story in your own words.

The Simpleton, p. 23. 1. What is a "simpleton"? 2. Where did Simpleton get his money? 3. What did he buy with it? 4. What did he do with the goose? 5. What does Act II tell you? 6. What does Act III tell you? 7. Why did Simpleton ask the king for a "sound" beating? 8. Act the story.

The Stone-Cutter, p. 30. 1. Why did the stone-cutter become discontented? 2. What wish did he make? 3. Who heard his wish and granted it? 4. Tell of other wishes the stone-cutter made. 5. Why was he discontented each time? 6. Why was Tawara happiest when he was a stone-cutter? 7. How would you answer Tawara's question in the last paragraph?

The Golden Fish, p. 34. 1. Find lines that show the fisherman was kind-hearted. 2. Why did his wife scold him when he returned from fishing? 3. How did the fish pay the fisherman for his kindness? 4. What had the fisherman's wife done that made the fish think she was not fit to rule others? 5. Why was the fisherman glad when the palace became a hut again? 6. Tell the story in your own words.

Brother Fox's Tar Baby, p. 40. 1. What does Act I tell you about Brother Rabbit? 2. Why did Brother Fox want to catch Brother Rabbit? 3. What plan did Brother Fox make for catching him? 4. Tell how Brother Rabbit got caught. 5. How did Brother Rabbit get free? 6. Dramatize the story.

———————

You have now read all the stories in the first part of the book. Which story did you think was the funniest? Which story taught the best lesson?

BROWNIES AND FAIRIES

In the happy land of "Make-Believe" live strange little folks—brownies and fairies and elves. The nicest of them all are the brownies, for they love to help anyone who has to work hard.

The stories and poems in this part of your reader will tell you about some of the funny things that happen in the land of "Make-Believe." When you have read all of these stories, tell the class which one gave you the best laugh, and which one you liked best.

The Brownie of Blednock, p. 47. 1. Why were the people frightened at the wee man? 2. Can you repeat the song that he sang as he went up the street? 3. What was Granny Duncan's advice? What did she mean by saying, "Handsome is, as handsome does"? 4. What were some of the good deeds Aiken-Drum did? 5. Why could he not stay in the village? 6. What strange saying of Aiken-Drum's did the people remember? 7. Tell the story, following this outline: (a) The wee man comes to town; (b) Granny Duncan's advice; (c) The brownie's good deeds; (d) Why Aiken-Drum left Blednock. 8. Use another word for "wages"; "tidy"; "glimpse"; "obliged"; "deeds."

The Fairies, p. 55. 1. What does the first stanza tell you about the fairies? 2. Where do some of them make their home? 3. What does the poet tell you of their watchdogs? 4. What would happen to anyone who dug up the thorn trees? 5. Read aloud the stanza that you like best. 6. Why is the mountain called "airy"?

How Doughnuts Came to Be Made, p. 57. 1. Tell how the little cook looked. 2. What did he cook for the fairy's dinner? 3. How did the fairy prove that she was a good cook? 4. How did the little cook get a wedding ring? 5. Tell the story in your own words.

The Fairy Shoes, p. 61. 1. What was the fairy godmother's gift? 2. Why were the fairy shoes wonderful? 3. What happened to Tim's brothers when they wore the fairy shoes? 4. Why did Tim's mother make him wear them? 5. What good plan did Tim discover that his brothers had not thought of? 6. What did Tim find when he reached his school? 7. Use another word for "parcel"; "cluster." 8. Tell the story in your own words.

The Brownies, p. 67. 1. What kind of boys were Johnnie and Tommy? 2. What did Tommy dream? 3. Read lines that tell what the boys decided to do, after Tommy had told Johnnie about his dream. 4. Did the boys really help their father by their work? 5. Who became the best brownie of all after a while?

The Jumblies, p. 75. 1. What tells you that this is a nonsense poem? 2. The poet, Edward Lear, "makes up" several nonsense words just for fun; what are some of these made-up words? 3. Which stanza gave you the best laugh? 4. Why would a sieve not make a good boat? 5. Use another word for "extremely"; "voyage."

The Skylark's Spurs, p. 77. 1. What showed that the fairy was unkind? 2. What did the fairy say the skylark did with his spurs? 3. How did the grasshopper comfort the skylark? 4. How did the skylark win a mate? 5. Where do larks make their nests? 6. What did the skylark find his spurs were for? 7. Tell the story in your own words.

Which story in this group did you like best? Why do you think the brownies are the nicest of the little folks who live in the land of "Make-Believe"?

Children

So far in this book you have read only about wonderful things that happened in a magic world. You have seen brownies and fairies and strange animals that knew how to talk.

But some of the poets and storytellers have written about real boys and girls like you. Most of the selections in the group you are now going to read are of this kind. Some of them will make you laugh; some of them will give you little pictures of children playing just as you often like to play; and some of them will show you how foolish it is to be always cross or careless or idle.

The most famous of these poets who wrote about real boys and girls was Robert Louis Stevenson. If you know any of his poems besides the ones given here, recite them to the class.

Farewell to the Farm, p. 85. 1. What tells you that the "eager" children are in the country? Why were they "eager"? 2. What do you see in the picture on page 85? 3. Where do you think the children are going? 4. What does the picture on page 86 suggest to you? 5. What does the poet mean by saying "the trees and houses smaller grow"?

A Good Play, p. 87. 1. Where was the ship built? 2. What did the children take with them to eat? 3. What word tells that they were to sail on big waves? 4. How long did they sail? Who was in the boat? 5. Who can read the poem so as to make us *see* the sailing party? 6. Who wrote this poem? What other poems by the same writer have you read?

The Princess Who Never Laughed, p. 88. 1. How did the first son treat the old man who asked him for food? How did the second son treat him? The third son? 2. What happened to each of them? 3. How was the third son rewarded for his kindness? 4. Tell the story in your own words.

The Golden Pears, p. 94. 1. On what errand was the oldest son sent? 2. How did he answer the witch that he met? 3. What happened when he reached the palace? 4. How did the second son answer the witch? 5. What happened to the second son? 6. What did the youngest son reply to the witch's question? 7. What did the witch do to help the youngest son? 8. How did the king reward the boy? 9. Find what the king said about telling the truth. 10. How did the king help the boys' father?

Which Loved Best? p. 103. 1. What did John love more than he loved his mother? 2. What did Nell love more than she loved her mother? 3. How did Fan show that she really loved her mother? 4. How do you think the mother knew which loved her best?

Irene, the Idle, p. 104. 1. What words of advice did the fairy give to Irene? 2. What requests did the fire, the woodbox, the floor, the cup, and the dishes make? 3. What was Irene's excuse to the fairy for the disorder of the house? 4. Read the fairy's reply. 5. What did Irene find that she must do? 6. Why was Irene's birthday such a happy one?

Suppose, p. 115. 1. In the first stanza, what advice does the poet give? In the second stanza? In the third? In the fourth? In the fifth? 2. Why do you think it is best always to be cheerful and sweet-tempered? 3. What words does the poet use to speak of a fine carriage drawn by two horses?

Which selection in this part of the book gave you the best laugh? Which selection gave you the best advice? Which selection did you think most interesting?

LEGENDS

Hundreds of years ago, people did not understand what made the stormy winds blow, or how flowers grow, or why spring comes after the long winter, or many other things that wise men today have learned. In that long-ago time people imagined that some magic king could tell the wind when to blow, and that a tall youth whom they called Spring came walking through the world when Winter had stayed too long.

The stories they told about these wonderful things are called legends, and many of them have come down to us from very early times. Some of the most interesting legends are those of the Greeks and the Indians.

Ulysses and the Bag of Winds, p. 119. 1. How long were Ulysses and his men away from home, fighting for their country? 2. On their way home, where did they stop to rest? 3. How did Aeolus help them? 4. Why did he leave the west wind out of the bag? 5. Who watched the bag of winds on the journey homeward? 6. Who untied the bag? Why? What happened? 7. Did Ulysses ever get back to his home?

The Star and the Lily, p. 123. 1. What dream did the young warrior have? 2. Why did the star not like its home in the white rose on the mountainside? 3. Why did it not like its prairie home? 4. What was the little "creature of the air" that the star lived with for a while on the prairie? 5. Why did the star choose to live upon the lake? 6. What flower did the star become when it came to live upon the lake? What did the Indians call it?

Peboan and Seegwun, p. 128. 1. What was the old Indian doing, as he sat in the wigwam? 2. What "great deeds" did he say he had done? 3. What great deeds did the tall young man say that he could do? 4. In the morning, what became of the old man? 5. Who was the old Indian? The young Indian? 6. What flower was seen where the old man's fire had been? 7. Why is this flower said to belong both to winter and to spring?

Which of these legends did you think was the most interesting? Commit to memory "Which Wind Is Best?"

HOLIDAYS

Once upon a time an old man named Scrooge was talking to his nephew, who had come to wish him a Merry Christmas. "Bah!" said the old man. "Keeping Christmas is a foolish custom. If I had my way, no one would be allowed to keep Christmas!" In fact, Scrooge would have done away with every holiday.

What a dull place this old world would be if Scrooge had been given his wish! Just think of three hundred and sixty-five days without any Thanksgiving or Christmas or New Year or Easter. Half the fun would go out of your life, wouldn't it?

But that is not the worst of it. If Christmas and Thanksgiving and Easter were no longer kept, we should lose many little acts of kindness that help make the world a better place in which to live.

As you read the stories in the "Holiday" part of this book, see which one tells of the happiest time; which one tells of the kindest act; and which one gives you the best laugh.

A Thanksgiving Fable, p. 131. 1. What did the hungry cat watch upon Thanksgiving morning? 2. What did the cat say? (Read the lines.) 3. What did the mouse do when she heard the cat's words? 4. Read the poem so as to bring out the fun of it. 5. What word does the poet use for "refused"? For "thought about" in the last stanza?

Little Pumpkin's Thanksgiving, p. 132. 1. What wish did the Little Wee Pumpkin make? 2. Tell how the Little Wee Pumpkin's wish came true. 3. How have you made someone happy at Thanksgiving time? 4. Tell the story in your own words.

A Christmas Wish, p. 137. 1. Why do you think the poet would like "a stocking made for a giant"? 2. Make a list of all the toys that the poet thinks children would want. 3. What other things does he say that they would want? 4. Use another word for "search"; "beasts"; "meeting-house." 5. What words does the poet use in the second stanza to tell of dishes that were just the kind a girl would like best?

Gretchen's Christmas, p. 139. 1. Why did the empty shoes make Gretchen's heart sad? 2. Which doll in the toy store window pleased Gretchen most? 3. What loving deeds did Margaret do on Christmas Eve? 4. What Christmas gift did Gretchen find when she awoke?

An Easter Surprise, p. 148. 1. What were the "round brown things" that Paul dug up in his mother's tulip bed? 2. What did Paul do with them? 3. Why did the little old lady think she would have no flower garden that year? 4. What happened to her flower bed, that surprised her? 5. Why were the little old lady and her husband so happy when they saw the tulips?

Which selection in this part of the book told of the kindest act? Which told of the happiest times? Which gave you the best laugh?

HOME AND COUNTRY

Have you ever watched a parade of soldiers going by, with the American flag flying proudly in the breeze as they marched? If you have, perhaps you thought that you would like to be a brave soldier some day, ready to fight for this great country of ours.

We hope that there will be no more wars for a long, long time to come, so that America may not need to ask you to fight her battles. But even if you never are a soldier for your country, you can do your part in making America the best country in all the world.

Perhaps you are wondering how a boy or girl can help to do so great a thing as this. Well, stop a moment and think what it is that makes a country great, that makes it the best kind of place to live in. Isn't it happy homes, and kind neighbors, and people who work faithfully and live simple, healthful lives? Surely every boy or girl can be a good little American by helping in things like these.

When you have read the first story in this part of your book, tell the class why people like Appleseed John make good Americans. When you have read "A Little Lad of Long Ago," tell the class why this young boy grew up to be one of the best Americans who ever lived. When you have read the other stories in this group, see how many ways you can think of for boys and girls to help America. Will buying Thrift Stamps help? Will kindness to animals and birds help? Will kind acts on Thanksgiving and Christmas help? Will being a good member of the Boy Scouts or the Camp Fire Girls help?

Appleseed John, p. 153. 1. What plan for helping others did the kind old man make? 2. What did the village people think of him? 3. What did the boys say of him? 4. What did the old man do with the apple cores that he saved? 5. How did the old man's work help others in later years?

Columbus and His Son, Diego, p. 158. 1. For what purpose did Columbus try to get ships? 2. Why did Columbus think that he might find help at the convent? What help did he get from one of the friars? 3. What did Columbus say he could prove? 4. Who gave Columbus ships and money for the voyage? 5. Where did Columbus leave his son, Diego, while he was away on the voyage? 6. How did the other pages tease Diego? 7. What did one of the pages call the Atlantic Ocean? 8. Why was Columbus called The Mad Sailor? 9. What message came from Columbus one day? 10. What did Columbus discover? 11. What had Columbus proved by his voyage? 12. Use another word for "voyage"; "aid"; "page"; "globe."

The Boy, the Bees, and the British, p. 165. 1. Tell why 1781 was a hard year in Virginia. 2. What did Jack wish to do? 3. Jack's mother told him why he had been left at home; read her words. 4. Who were the "redcoats"? 5. Tell about the coming of the redcoats to the plantation. 6. Why was Jack glad that he was at home? 7. What daring plan did Jack think of? How did he make the bees fight the British? 8. After he had thrown the bee-hive at the soldiers, what did he do? 9. Do you think Jack found a good way to help his country even though he was too young to join Washington's army? 10. Use another word for "seizing"; "plantation"; "clump."

Why Jimmie Missed the Parade, p. 171. 1. In what parade were the boy scouts to take part? 2. What soldiers were to be in the parade? 3. Recite from memory the lines Jimmie had learned from Margaret Sangster's beautiful poem about George Washington. 4. Why did Jimmie miss the parade?

5. What happened at the scout meeting that night? 6. What other stories of kindness and helpfulness have you read in this book? 7. Use another word for "forming"; "blast"; "stunned"; "crushed." 8. What words does the poet use for "birthday" in the lines Jimmie learned? For "spoken of"?

A Little Lad of Long Ago, p. 176. 1. Why was little Abe called a funny-looking boy? 2. Why does the story say you would have liked him? 3. Why was the borrowed book so precious to little Abe? 4. Why did the boy read the book at night, instead of in daytime? 5. Where did he put the book each night when he had finished reading it? 6. What happened to the book one night? 7. What did little Abe do at once when he saw the book was spoiled? 8. Do you think he acted in a manly way by going to the owner? 9. How did the boy earn the right to keep the book? 10. Can you give the name of the book? 11. What did Abraham Lincoln say about this book, after he had become president of the United States? 12. Use another word for "clumsy"; "chinks."

Jacques, a Red Cross Dog, p. 180. 1. In this story who is telling of his life on the farm? 2. Tell in your own words of Jacques's life on the little farm in France. 3. Tell of Jacques's training at the war-dog school. 4. Tell how Jacques saved his master. 5. Jacques was "decorated" several times, that is, he was given medals or ribbons as a reward for his bravery. Did these decorations make him proud? 6. What was the only thing Jacques was proud of? 7. What do the words "sent to the front" mean, on page 185?

Why is it a good thing to read stories about Washington, Lincoln, and others who have helped our country? Can you tell the class any story about some other American who helped our country? What are some of the ways in which you can show that you are a good American?

Heroes of Long Ago

Perhaps you have read, in fairy tales, of heroes who killed dragons or saved fair ladies from death. But here are three stories about *real* heroes, who lived long ago.

One of them, Joseph, was a wise ruler who saved his people from starving; another of them, David, was a great soldier who wrote wonderful songs; and the third, Saint George, did many brave deeds as he went about helping people who were in trouble. The dragon that is told of in this story of Saint George was probably some great beast.

Suggestions for Silent Reading

(a) All of the stories in this group, as well as several other stories in other parts of this book, may be read silently in preparing for the class period. The recitation may then be given to testing how well you have read, and to the reading aloud of selected parts of stories.

(b) In preparing your lesson, read the story silently as rapidly as you can, but not so fast that you fail to get the thought. In silent reading remember that pointing to the words with your fingers or reading with your lips slows your speed. Try constantly to increase your speed in silent reading.

(c) Test yourself, *first*, by seeing how many of the questions you can answer after reading the story once; and, *second*, by telling the main thoughts of the story. You may need to read the story again to be able to answer all the questions and to tell the story completely.

Joseph, the Ruler, p. 189. 1. Which of Joseph's older brothers was kind to him? 2. Why did the others hate him? 3. How did the wicked brothers get rid of Joseph? 4. How did the king of Egypt show that he believed Joseph was good and wise? 5. Why did Joseph's brothers go to Egypt? 6. How did Joseph treat his brothers when they came to buy corn? (Wheat was known as "corn" in Joseph's time.) 7. What made Joseph the happiest man in Egypt? 8. *Class readings:* the conversation on pages 190, 191 (five pupils); Joseph's dream, page 191 (two pupils); the meaning of the dream, pages 193, 194 (three pupils); Joseph forgives his brothers, pages 197 to 199 (eleven pupils).

David, the Singer, p. 200. 1. What was David's work when he was a boy? 2. Tell some things which David had to do that you would like to do; what part of his work would you not like? 3. With what did David fight the lion? 4. How did he fight the band of robbers? 5. How did David help King Saul? 6. For what is David remembered? 7. *Class readings:* the conversation between David and his mother, pages 200, 201; the conversation on pages 203, 204, 205.; the conversation on pages 206, 207, 208.

Saint George and the Dragon, p. 211. 1. What story did the plowman tell George? 2. When George had grown tall and strong, what did he ask the queen to allow him to do? 3. Why did she not want to send George to fight the dragon? 4. What brave deed did George do in the Wandering Wood? 5. Why was the giant able to take George prisoner? 6. How was George saved from the giant? 7. How did the wise old man comfort him? 8. How has George's brave life helped other boys? 9. *Class readings:* the conversation on pages 214, 215, 216 (three pupils); the wise man's words, page 217; the last three paragraphs on page 219.

Can you tell the class of an American in World War One who was like Joseph because he saved thousands of people from starving? What other Americans do you know of who are famous because they were great soldiers, or because they helped our people in some way?

The Outdoor World

"Oh, wouldn't it be nice, Aunt Molly, if there really were fairies!" said a little girl in one of the stories you are now going to read.

"Are you quite sure there is no Fairyland?" asked Aunt Molly. And then she showed the little girl some of the wonderful things that were happening all around her in the great outdoor world. Yes, this big world of ours, with its animals and birds and flowers, is really a sort of fairyland, if only we keep our eyes wide open to see.

As you read the stories and poems in this part of your book, see how many wonderful things you notice that prove Aunt Molly was right.

My Chickadee Guests, p. 220. 1. Who is talking in this story? 2. How do you know that the author loves birds? 3. Which of the birds mentioned in this story have you seen? 4. Tell in your own words about the author's five chickadee guests at breakfast. 5. Listen while a good reader reads the story aloud. 6. Use another word for "ledge"; "certainly."

Brother Green-Coat, p. 227. 1. Why did Betty wish that there were elves and fairies? 2. Read aloud the conversation between Aunt Molly and Betty, pages 228, 229 (two pupils). 3. Tell how Aunt Molly's little friend looked each time she saw him. 4. What was the name of her little friend? 5. What is Brother Green-Coat's name before he puts on his velvet suit? 6. Where does Brother Green-Coat live in winter? 7. What did

Betty learn from Aunt Molly's little friend? 8. Read aloud the conversation on pages 231, 232 (two pupils). 9. In the picture on page 232, point to the frog's eggs; the tadpoles.

What Kept the Chimney Waiting, p. 235. 1. Why were the boys glad when they heard that a new chimney was to be built? 2. What did the grandfather show the boys, that explained why the new chimney had to wait? 3. What is thistle-down?

Nest Eggs, p. 238. 1. Where was the nest built? 2. What can the little birds do that the children, though older, cannot do? 3. Who wrote this poem? What other poems by the same author have you read in this book? 4. Recite from memory any poem by Stevenson that you know. 5. Explain: "in the fork"; "frail eggs"; "tops of the beeches."

Jack Frost and the Pitcher, p. 242. 1. Why did Jack Frost say that Katrina was careless? 2. Why did he not go into the sitting room? 3. What happened to the pitcher? 4. What was Katrina doing while Jack Frost was busy? 5. Use another word for "creaked"; "chuckled"; "glowing"; "glide." 6. *Class readings;* the conversation between Katrina and her mother, pages 242, 243 (two pupils); the last two paragraphs on page 246.

Mother Spider, p. 248. 1. Which of the little creatures mentioned on page 248 have you seen? 2. What did Mother Spider carry in her mouth this summer day? 3. What was in her white bag? 4. What did she carry on her back at a later time, when Grasshopper Green met her? 5. Use another word for "pounced." 6. Read the conversation between Mother Spider and Grasshopper Green (two pupils).

———————

What did you learn from the last story that makes you think Aunt Molly was right when she told Betty that some of us live in Fairyland without knowing it? Which story in this part of the book did you like best?

OLD TALES

And now we come to the very last part of our book. Here you will find some of the famous old fairy tales that have been told over and over in many different countries. No doubt your mother, when she was a little girl, loved to read about the Sleeping Beauty and about Cinderella. Very likely your grandmother, too, loved these stories, and her mother and grandmother, before her.

When you have read these stories, see if you can tell why they have been told in so many lands and for so long a time.

The Sleeping Beauty, p. 252.* 1. Why did the king invite only twelve of the fairies to the feast? 2. What did the wicked fairy do? 3. What was the twelfth fairy's gift? 4. Tell what happened to the maiden on the day she became fifteen. 5. Read lines that tell of this deep sleep that fell upon the whole palace. 6. What were the words of the young prince when he heard the story of the enchanted castle? 7. How did he wake the princess?

Cinderella, p. 258.* 1. Why was the youngest of the sisters called Cinderella? 2. Tell of Cinderella's two sisters and their mother. 3. How did her fairy godmother prepare Cinderella to go to the ball? 4. At what time was Cinderella to return home? 5. How was she received at the ball? 6. Why did Cinderella wish to go to the ball again on the next night? 7. What happened when the clock struck twelve? 8. How did the prince find the owner of the little glass slipper? 9. Find lines which show that Cinderella forgave her sisters for their unkind treatment of

---

* See "Suggestions for Silent Reading," page 308.

her. 10. Tell the story of Cinderella, following this outline: (a) Cinderella's selfish sisters; (b) The fairy godmother; (c) Cinderella at the ball; (d) The glass slipper.

Hans and the Four Great Giants, p. 271.* 1. What kind of boy was Hans? 2. Why did he go out to find work? 3. Why did Hans go in search of the enchanted pearls? 4. Tell of his trip to the North Sea. 5. How did Hans win the princess? 6. Do you think he deserved his good fortune? 7. Read lines which show that Hans was grateful. 8. Tell the story, following this outline: (a) Hans goes out into the world; (b) The enchanted pearls; (e) Hans wins the princess. 9. *Class readings:* the conversation between Hans and the four giants, pages 273, 274, 275, 276, 277 (five pupils); Hans wins the princess, pages 278, 279.

The Ugly Duckling, p. 280.* 1. How did the mother duck find out that the ugly little one was not a turkey? 2. Why was the duckling not liked in the farmyard or in the hut? 3. Why did the duckling wish to be beautiful? 4. Do you think the duckling would have been called "ugly" if he had always lived with the swans? 5. Read lines that tell how happy the duckling was when he was called beautiful. 6. Use another word for "handsome"; "plunge"; "reeds"; "slender"; "image." 7. Tell the story, following this outline: (a) The great egg; (b) In the farmyard; (c) In the hut; (d) The beautiful swan. 8. *Class readings:* the conversation between the mother duck and the friendly duck, page 281; the conversation of the mother duck and the Spanish duck, page 284; the conversation in the hut, pages 286, 287, 288, 289 (four pupils).

Which story in this group did you like best? Which story did you like best in the entire book? Which poem in this book do you like best? Recite from memory any lines of poetry you have memorized from this book.

---

* See "Suggestions for Silent Reading," page 308.

WORD LIST

a as in m<u>a</u>t   ə as in b<u>a</u>nana   ä as in f<u>a</u>ther   ∅ as in s<u>i</u>de
e as in b<u>e</u>d   ər as in f<u>ur</u>ther   aů as in l<u>ou</u>d   ŋ as in si<u>ng</u>
i as in t<u>i</u>p   ā as in d<u>ay</u>   ē as in n<u>ee</u>d   ō as in sn<u>o</u>w
ȯ as in s<u>aw</u>   ȯi as in c<u>oin</u>   ü as in r<u>u</u>le   ů as in p<u>u</u>ll
ᵊ as in eat<u>e</u>n   th as in hea<u>th</u>er

A

act ('akt) part

ac tive ('ak-tiv) quick; nimble

ad ven ture (ad-ven-'ture) a remarkable happening

Aeolus ('ē-ə-ləs)

aid ('ād) help

Ai ken Drum ('ā-kən)

Aire dales ('ar-dəlz) a kind of dog

air y ('ar-ē) breezy

a light (ə-'l∅t) come to rest

al li ga tor ('a-lə-gā-tər) a large animal that lives in the water

all to her mind of just the kind she liked

al mond ('ä-mənd) a nut

al tered ('ȯl-tərd) changed

am bu lance ('am-byə-ləns) long covered car in which wounded men are carried

a mus ing (a-'myü-ziŋ) funny

anx ious ly ('aŋk-shəs-lē) eagerly

ar bor-like ('är-bər-l∅k) like a shelter made of vines or trees

ar bu tus (är-'byü-təs) an early spring flower

ar gue ('är-gyü) try to make her change her mind

ar mor ('är-mər) metal covering worn to protect the body in battle

a slant (ə-'slant) on one side

at any rate well; at least

at tend (ə-'tend) heed; care for

au tumn ('ȯ-təm) fall

315

awk ward ('ȯ-kwerd) clumsy

B

bade ('bād) ordered; told

ball ('bȯl) fine party with dancing

band ('band) several together

banks ('baŋks) sides of earth or rock

bare ('bar) leafless; without grass

beak ('bēk) bill

beat ('bēt) get ahead of

be cause (bi-'kȯz)

beech ('bēch) a kind of tree

beloved (be-'lə-vəd) dear; loved

Beth le hem ('beth-lə-hem)

bil lows ('bi-lōz) great waves

bitterly ('bi-tər-li) painfully; hard

blast ('blast) long note

bleat ('blēt) noise made by sheep

Bled nock ('bled-näk)

bloom ('blüm) blossom

boast ('bōst) brag

bold ly ('bōld-lē) as if he were not afraid

bore ('bōr) endured; lived; held

boughs ('baus) branches

bowed ('baud) bend

brains ('brānz) wise thoughts

breast knot ('brest-nät) feathers on the breast

brisk ('brisk) quick; lively

bris tling ('bris-liŋ) angry; threatening

bronze ('bränz) a reddish metal

budge ('bəj) move

bur dock ('bər-däk) a common weed

burst ('berst) come suddenly

busi ness ('biz-nəs) what one has to do

butt ('bət) strike with the head

C

Ca naan ('kā-nən)

cap ture ('kap-chər) take by force

car a van ('kar-ə-van) a number of people traveling together

car ol ('kar-əl) song of praise; Christmas hymn; sing

cer tain ly ('sər-tən-lē) surely

Chank ly Bore ('chank-lē; 'bōr)

charge ('chärj) a duty or task given one to do

char i ot ('char-ē-ət) a kind of carriage

charm ing ('chär-miŋ) pleasing; beautiful; delightful

cheat ed ('chē-təd) fooled

chil ly ('chi-lē) cold

chink ('chiŋk) crack

chip ('chip) break open

chis el ('chi-zəl) long, sharp tool

chris ten ing ('kris-niŋ) church service where a baby is named

chuck le ('chə-kəl) laugh to oneself

churn ('chərn) tub or jar for making butter; stir; beat

cin ders ('sin-dərz) ashes

claimed ('klāmd) said he had a right to

clasped ('klaspt) took hold of and held firmly

clat ter ('kla-tər) rattling noise

clev er ('kle-vər) sharp; cunning

cling ('kliŋ) hold fast

cloak ('klōk) loose coat

clump ('kləmp) group of bushes or trees

clum sy ('kləm-zē) awkward

clus ter ('kləs-tər) bunch

coach and pair ('kōch; 'pār) fine carriage drawn by two horses

coach man ('kōch-man) driver

cock ('käk) rooster

col lie ('kä-lē) large, shepherd dog

com fort ('kəm-fərt) cheer

com i cal ('kä-mi-kəl) laughable

com mand (kə-'mand) order; control; rule

com plain (kəm-'plān) find fault; grumble
con cealed (kən-'sēld) hidden
con fused (kən-'fyüz) bothered so they could not think clearly
con stant ('kän-stənt) going on all the time
con tent ed (kən-'ten-təd) satisfied
con ven ient (kən-'vēn-yənt) easy; handy
con vent ('kän-vənt) home of monks or nuns
Co sette (kō-'zet)
covert ('kō-vərt) shelter; hiding place
crag gy ('kra-gē) covered with rough, broken rocks
creaked ('krēkt) squeaked
cre a tion (krē-'ā-shən) world, sun, moon, and stars
crea ture ('krē-chər) any live thing
crisp ('krisp) thin and dry; easily broken
croak ing ('krō-kiŋ) a frog's cry
crushed ('krəsht) mashed
cuckoo ('kü-kü) a brown bird
curb ('kərb) edge of the sidewalk next to the street
curious flight ('kyur-ē-əs) strange way of flying
curt sied ('kərt-sēd) bowed

D

dain ty ('dān-tē) delicate; pleasant; something good to eai
daren't ('dar-ənt) do not dare
dar ing ('dar-iŋ) bold
dawn ('dȯn) daybreak
de clined (di-'klȱnd) refused
deed ('dēd) act
de lay (di-'lā) put off; waste time; make lose time
de li cious (de-'li-shəs) delightful; pleasing to the taste
de light (di-'lȱt) happiness; joy
de light ful (di-'lȱt-fəl) very pleasant
dell ('del) small valley
den ('den) home of a wild animal
dew y ('dü-ē) wet with dew
Di e go (dē-'ā-gō)

dim pled ('dim-pəld) having little hollows like dimples
dis ap peared (di-sə-'pird) went out of sight
dis cour aged (dis-'ker-ijd) be discouraged, lose heart; give up
down ('daùn) soft, fluffy feathers
drag on ('dra-gən) an imagined creature of great fierce-ness
droop ('drüp) bend over
duck ling ('dek-liŋ) little duck
dumb ('dəm) quiet
dunce ('dəns) stupid person
dusk ('dəsk) dim light just before dark
dwarf ('dwòrf) a tiny person

E

ea ger ('ē-gər) ready to do or go
ear nest ('ər-nəst) thoughtful; serious
ef fect (i-'fekt) result
ef fort ('e-fərt) attempt
E gypt ('i-jipt)
elf ('elf) a fairy
en chant ed (in-'chan-təd) magic
en rolled (in-'rōld) put on the list
ere ('er) before
ev er more (e-vər-'mōr) always; forever
evil ('ē-vəl) wrongdoing; wrong
ex press (ik-'spres) tell
ex treme ly (ik-'strēm-lē) very

F

faint ('fānt) not bright or plain; weak
fair ('far) pretty; good-looking; sweet
faith ful ('fāth-fəl) true; steady
fam ine ('fa-mən) need of food
fared ('fard) got along
fare well (far-'wel) good-bye
fash ioned ('fa-shənd) made
fate ('fāt) fortune; unhappy end

fa vor ite ('fā-və-rət) liked more than another

fierce ('firs) furious; violent

fi er y ('fØ-ə-rē) looking like fire

firm ('fərm) without moving at all

firmly ('fərm-lē) tightly

flat ter ('fla-tər) please with praise which is not true

flax ('flaks) the fiber of the plant from which linen is made

fled ('fled) ran away

fleece ('flēs) sheep's wool

fleecy ('flē-sē) like the wool of a sheep

flight ('flØt) flying; way of flying

flit ('flit) fly quickly

flung ('flung) threw quickly

flut ter ('flə-tər) move about excitedly; wave back and forth; fly

fod der-corn ('fä-dər) dry cornstalks

folk ('fōk) people

footmen ('füt-mən) men servants

for est ('fòr-əst) thick woods

fork ('fòrk) place where a large branch parts into two smaller ones .

form ing ('fòr-miŋ) getting ready to march

for tune ('fòr-chən) success; luck

for ward ('fòr-wərd) ahead

fox glove ('fäks-gləv) a kind of flower growing along a high stalk

frail ('frā-əl) easily broken; weak

Fran çois (fran-'swä)

fret ful ('fret-fəl) likely to cry

fri ar ('frØ-ər) a kind of monk

frock ('fräk) dress

front ('frənt) battle line where the fighting goes on

fros ty ('frò-stē) covered with frost

fur nish ings ('fer-nish-iŋz) furniture and decorations

fur rows ('fər-ōs) open spaces between the rows

G

gar den er ('gär-dən-ər) one who works in a garden

gar land ('gär-lənd) wreath

gar ment ('gär-mənt) dress; clothing

gath er ('ga-thər) draw close

gay ('gā) happy; bright; joyful

glade ('glād) open place in a wood

glance ('glans) quick look

gleam ('glēm) flash; shine

glen ('glen) narrow valley

glide ('glØd) move smoothly along

glimpse ('glimps) a quick sight

glit ter ing ('gli-tə-riŋ) shining

globe ('glōb) ball; sphere

glow ('glō) brightness; shine

god moth er ('gäd-mə-thər) a woman who promises when a child is christened to help it

good-na tured ly (gùd-'nā-chərd-lē) kindly

good-temp ered (gùd-'təm-pərd) pleasant; kind

grace ful ly ('grās-fə-lē) with light pretty movements

grant ('grant) allow; permit

grasped ('graspt) took hold of

Greek ('grēk) living in Greece

greet ('grēt) welcome

grief ('grēf) sorrow; distress

grim ('grim) fierce; stern

gros beak ('grōs-bēk) a bird with a large thick bill

ground ('graùnd) pressed hard

guard ('gärd) protect from danger; defend

H

hand ker chief ('haŋ-kər-chəf)

hand some ('han-səm) good-looking; **handsome is as handsome does**, how you act matters more than how you look

hare ('har) rabbit

haste ('hāst) hurry

has ten ('hā-sən) hurry
hearth ('härth) fireplace
heart y ('här-tē) great; cheerful
hedge ('hej) fence of bushes
hedge hog ('hej-hȯg) a small animal covered with prickles
heed ('hēd) pay attention to
helmet ('hel-mət) a covering for the head in battle
hel ter skel ter ('hel-tər; 'skel-tər) in hurry and disorder
hob gob lin ('häb-gäb-lən) mischievous elf or goblin; brownie
home spun (hōm-'spən) woven at home; coarse; plain
hon or ('ä-nər) respect; sign of favor
hor ri ble ('hȯr-ə-bəl) shocking; terrible
hos pi tal ('häs-pi-təl) a place in which sick people are cared for
host ('hōst) a great number
huge ('hyüj) very large; great
hurled ('hər-əld) thrown hard
hut ('hət) poor, small house

I

ill-tem pered (il-'tem-pərd) cross
im age ('i-mij) picture
inn ('in) hotel
in stant ly ('in-stənt-lē) that very minute
in sult ('in-səlt) be very rude to
in tend ed (in-'ten-dəd) planned
in ter rupt (in-tə-'rəpt) talk when some one else is talking
Is ra el ('iz-rē-əl) the Hebrews; the Jewish people

J

jack daw ('jak-dȯ) a black bird
Jacques ('zhak)
Japan (jə-'pan) the group of islands east of Asia
Jeanne ('zhan)
jin gling ('jiŋ-gliŋ) rattling
jol li est ('jä-lē-əst) gayest
jolt ('jōlt) jerk

jos tle ('jä-səl) push and crowd
jour ney ('jer-nē) trip
joy ful ly ('jȯi-fə-lē) happily; very gladly

K

Kat ri na (ka-'trē-na)
keep er ('kē-per) one who guards or takes care of
ker nel ('kər-nəl) inside part which we eat
knight ('nΦt) man who had promised to help any who were
  in trouble

L

lan guage ('lan-gwij) speech
lau rel ('lȯr-əl) an evergreen tree or shrub
lawn ('lȯn) ground covered with grass
leaped ('lēpt) jumped
leath er y ('le-thə-rē) dry, tough
ledge ('lej) little outside shelf
leg end ('le-jənd) old story
lin ger ('liŋ-gər) stay or wait long; go slowly
liz ard ('li-zərd) a little creeping animal
loi ter ('lȯi-tər) move slowly; stop to play
lol li pop ('lä-li-päp) a kind of candy
long ing ('lȯŋ-iŋ) wishing very much
look out ('lu̇k-au̇t) watch; one who watches
lot ('lät) fortune; fate
lowed ('lōd) mooed softly

M

mac a roon ('mak-ə-rün) a small cake
mal let ('ma-lət) wooden hammer
man aged ('ma-nijd) done
Man i tou ('ma-nə-tu̇) the Indian name for God
marsh ('märsh) soft wet land partly covered with water
marsh mar i gold ('märsh; 'mar-ə-gōld) a yellow flower that
  grows in wet places
mate ('māt) wife; companion
mea dow ('me-dō) grassy field
meet ing house ('mēt-iŋ 'hau̇s) church

mel low ('me-lō) ripe
mer chant ('mər-chənt) man who buys and sells
mer ry ('mer-ē) jolly
might y ('mØt-ē) powerful
mild ('mØld) gentle; kind
mill ('mil) place where grain is ground
mil let ('mi-lət) a kind of grass
mind ('mØnd) tend; object to
mis chief ('mis-chəf) harm
mi ser ('mØ-zər) one who has riches but lives poorly
moc ca sin ('mä-kə-sən) loose shoe made of one piece of leather
mon ster ('män-stər) strange or horrible animal
mor tar ('mȯr-tər) lime mixed with sand and water
moss es ('mȯ-səz) tiny, soft green plants
moun ting ('mäun-tiŋ) climbing; getting upon
mourn ('mōrn) be sorry; grieve
mur mur ('mər-mər) make a low sound
muse ('myüz) think about

N

Nan nette (na-'net)
na tal ('nā-təl) of birth
nay ('nā) no
ne'er ('nar) never
neigh bor ('nā-bər) one who lives near another
neighed ('nād) whinnied
nip ('nip) bite off
no ble ('nō-bəl) splendid; very fine
nook ('nủk) little spot

O

o be di ent (ō-'bē-dē-ənt) doing what one is told to do
o bliged (ō-'blijd) forced; bound
o'er ('ōr) over; past
old en ('ōl-dən) very old; long ago
o ri ole ('ōr-ē-ōl) a small black and orange-colored bird
o ver come (ō-vər-'kəm) gain victory over; got over

o ver flowed (ō-vər-'flōd) rose above
overtake (ō-vər-'tāk) catch up with
oxhide ('äks-hØd) leather made from the skin of an ox

P

page ('pāj) boy who waited upon the people in the palace
Pa los ('pa-lōs)
pa poose (pa-'püs) Indian baby
par cel ('pär-səl) bundle; package
pas ture ('pas-chər) grassy place
patch ('pach) garden; spot
pa tient ly ('pā-shənt-lē) without complaint
pat ty ('pa-tē) small pie
Pe bo an ('pē-bō-an)
peer ('pir) look curiously
Pe rez ('per-əs)
per fect ly ('pər-fikt-lē) entirely; exactly
perk ('pərk) straighten up; show off
pet al ('pe-t°l) one of the small leaves which make up a
   flower
pe wee ('pē-wē) a little greenish gray bird
pierce ('pirs) make a way through
plain ('plān) clear; simple; not rich; a level country
plan ta tion (plan-'tā-shən) farm
plead ('plēd) ask earnestly; beg; offer as excuse
plen ti ful ('plen-ti-fəl) full; rich; having enough
plod ('pläd) walk heavily and slowly
plunge ('plənj) dive into; fall; jump
point ('pòint) little thing
pol ish ('pä-lesh) rub until they shine; make smooth or
   shiny
po si tion (pə-'zi-shən) place
pounce ('paůns) jump quickly
pranc ing ('pran-siŋ) springing
pray ('prā) beg; please
prec ious ('pre-shəs) of great value
pre fer ('pri-fər) like better; rather have

pre pare (pri-'par) make ready
pres ent ly ('pre-zᵊnt-lē) soon; after a while
pressed ('prest) ironed flat
prompt ('prämpt) ready quick; on time
prop er ('prä-pər) own; which belongs to it
psalm ('säm) a sacred song or poem
pump kin ('pəmp-kəm)
puz zled ('pə-zəld) confused

R

rage ('rāj) great anger
rays ('rāz) beams of light
rear ing ('rir-iŋ) jumping around
re count ed (rē-'kaȯn-təd) told again and again
red poll ('red-pōl) a small bird with a red head
reed ('rēd) tall grass growing in water
re gain (ri-'gān) get back
re joiced (ri-'jȯist) was glad
re quest (ri-'kwest) thing asked
res cued ('res-kyüd) freed; helped out of trouble
re ward (re-'wərd) pay for doing something
rich ('rich) fancy; costly; wealthy
rind ('r∅nd) outer hard skin
ring-bo ree ('riŋ-bō-rē)
rip en ing ('r∅-pə-niŋ) becoming ripe
robe ('rōb) flowing dress; decorations
rooks ('rȯks) large black birds
rough ('rəf) not well drawn
roy al ('rȯi-əl) such as a king might have
rud dy ('rə-dē) red
Ru pert ('rü-pərt)
rush y ('rə-shē) full of rushes—plants growing in wet
  places
rus set ('rə-sət) brown because dried up
rut ('rət) track worn by wheels

S

sad dles ('sa-dᵊlz) blankets with pockets

sat is fied ('sa-təs-fØd) contented; happy

saucy ('sȯ-sē) rude in a good-natured way

scant y ('skan-tē) very small; not enough

scorch ing ('skȯr-chiŋ) burning

scorn ('skȯrn) lack of respect

scram ble ('skram-bəl) climb on his hands and knees

scuf fling ('skə-fə-liŋ) good-natured rough play

sea foam ('sē; 'fōm) white mass of tiny bubbles on the shore

search ('sərch) hunt; look for

Seeg wun ('sēg-wən)

seize ('sēz) grab; take by force

sen ti nel ('sent-ᵊn-əl) soldier who watches while others sleep

serve ('sərv) work for; wait upon; do things for others; treat

sheaves ('shēvs) bundles

shep herd ('she-pərd) one who tends sheep

shield ('shēld) a frame of metal or wood carried on the arm in battle to keep off blows

shiv er ed ('shi-vərd) trembled

shrill ('shril) high and sharp

shud der ('shə-dər) tremble; shiver; trembling

shy ('shØ) timid

sieve ('siv) a sifter

si lence ('sØ-ləns) quiet

si lent ly ('sØ-lənt-lē) quietly

sim ple ton ('sim-pəl-tən) silly person

sis kin ('sis-kən) small bird

slen der ('slen-dər) long and slim

slum ber ('sləm-bər) sleep

sly ('slØ) tricky; cunning

snug ('snəg) cozy; comfortable

snug gle ('snə-gəl) cuddle

sound ('sau̇nd) hard.

spare ('spar) more than enough; give up; **spare room** bedroom kept for company

spark led ('spär-kəld) shone; twinkled

speech less ('spēch-ləs) unable to speak

spell ('spel) magic charm

spin dle ('spin-dᵊl) a round pointed stick with a notch to hold the yarn while spinning

spite ('spØt) ill will; meanness

splen did ('splen-dəd) very fine; grand; glorious

spray ('sprā) little branch

sprin kled ('spriŋ-kəld) scattered

squint ('skwint) partly close his eyes in trying to see better

squirm ('skərm) twist about; wriggle

stack ('stak) pile up

staff ('staf) long stick

stared ('stard) looked suprised

steals ('stēlz) walks carefully

steer ('stir) turn their flight

Stef an ('ste-fən)

store house ('stōr-haủs) building where things are put away

stream ('strēm) river or creek; shine straight in

stretch er bear ers ('stre-chər; 'bar-ərz) men who carry wounded on stretchers

strug gle ('strə-gəl) work hard; fight

stu dy ('stə-dē) room where one studies

stunned ('stənd) senseless; unable to move

stu pid ('stü-pəd) dull; foolish

suc cess (sək-'ses) good results

su et ('sü-ət) beef fat

swamp ('swämp) wet, low ground

swan ('swän) large, white bird

swarmed ('swȯrmd) seemed to be many and all moving in different ways

sway ing ('swā-iŋ) moving gently

swift ('swift) very quick; fast

T

task ('task) work; lesson

tat tered ('ta-tərd) ragged

Ta wa ra (ta-'wa-ra)

tend ed ('ten-dəd) took care of

ten der ly ('ten-dər-lē) gently; lovingly

ter ri er ('ter-ē-ər) a small dog

test ('test) examine; try

this tle down ('thi-səl-daủn) the soft, feathery, ripe thistle

throne room ('thrōn-rüm) room where the king meets his visitors

ti dings ('tɵ-diŋz) news

ti dy ('tɵ-dē) neat; put in order

tilt ('tilt) seesaw

Tor ri ble Zone ('tỏr-ə-bəl; 'zōn)

to ward ('tō-ərd) in the direction of

trav el er ('tra-və-lər) person going from one place to another

treas ure ('tre-zhər) riches; things of great value

treat ('trēt) something which gives great pleasure; deal with

trem bling ('trem-bə-liŋ) shaking

trench es ('tren-chəz) long, deep ditches in which men fought

troop ('trüp) move in crowds; large number

trou bled ('trə-bəld) worried

tru ant ('trü-ənt) one who stays away from school when one should go

twin kle ('twiŋ-kəl) gleam; look

U

U lys ses (yủ-'li-sēz)

un self ish ness (ən-'sel-fish-nəs) care and thought for others

up ris ing (əp-'rɵ-ziŋ) flying up

up roar ('əp-rōr) great noise

ut most ('ət-mōst) greatest

V

vale ('vāl) little valley

val ley ('va-lē) low ground between hills
veil ('vāl) very thin scarf
vic to ry ('vik-tə-rē) winning of a battle; success in a fight
voy age ('vȯi-ij) trip on the sea

W

wa ges ('wā-jəz) pay for work
wal let ('wä-lət) bag
wand ('wänd) fairy's magic stick
wan der ('wän-dər) walk about
warb ler ('wȯr-blər) a small song bird
war rior ('wȯr-ē-ər) soldier
weep ('wēp) cry
whip poor will ('hwi-pər-wil) a bird named from its call
whirl ('hwərl) turn round quickly; drive
wig wam ('wig-wäm) Indian but or tent
will ful ('wil-fəl) fond of his own way
won der ('wən-dər) surprise: woodland land covered with trees
wood land ('wu̇d-lənd) land covered with trees

Y

yon ('yän) that
Your Majesty ('yōr; 'ma-jə-stē) a polite name for the king

Books Available from
Lost Classics Book Company
American History
Stories of Great Americans for Little Americans..Edward Eggleston
A First Book in American History ....Edward Eggleston
A History of the United States and Its People ....Edward Eggleston
Biography
The Life of Kit Carson ....Edward Ellis
English Grammar
Primary Language Lessons.. Emma Serl
Intermediate Language Lessons .... Emma Serl
(*Teacher's Guides available for each of these texts*)
Elson Readers Series
Complete Set ....William Elson, Lura Runkel, Christine Keck
The Elson Readers: Primer......................William Elson, Lura Runkel
The Elson Readers: Book One...................William Elson, Lura Runkel
The Elson Readers: Book Two...................William Elson, Lura Runkel
The Elson Readers: Book Three.................................... William Elson
The Elson Readers: Book Four .... William Elson
The Elson Readers: Book Five ....William Elson, Christine Keck
The Elson Readers: Book Six ....William Elson, Christine Keck
The Elson Readers: Book Seven............William Elson, Christine Keck
The Elson Readers: Book Eight.............William Elson, Christine Keck
(*Teacher's Guides available for each reader in this series*)
Historical Fiction
With Lee in Virginia .... G. A. Henty
A Tale of the Western Plains .... G. A. Henty
The Young Carthaginian .... G. A. Henty
In the Heart of the Rockies.. G. A. Henty
For the Temple .... G. A. Henty
A Knight of the White Cross .... G. A. Henty
The Minute Boys of Lexington...........................Edward Stratemeyer
The Minute Boys of Bunker Hill........................Edward Stratemeyer
Hope and Have..Oliver Optic
Taken by the Enemy, First in *The Blue and the Gray Series* ....Oliver Optic
Within the Enemy's Lines, Second in *The Blue and the Gray Series* ..Oliver Optic
On the Blockade, Third in *The Blue and the Gray Series* ....Oliver Optic
Stand by the Union, Fourth in *The Blue and the Gray Series*..............Oliver Optic
Fighting for the Right, Fifth in *The Blue and the Gray Series*............Oliver Optic
A Victorious Union, Sixth and Final in *The Blue and the Gray Series* .....Oliver Optic
Mary of Plymouth ....James Otis

For more information visit us at: http://www.lostclassicsbooks.com